If the walls of Stockwell Mansion could talk...

The stories we could tell! To describe the Stockwell family dynasty as merely "interesting" is like calling this forty-room showplace "a house." Just wouldn't do the truth justice, now, would it? So let's talk about truth, shall we? Something that has been in short supply at times around here. Caine Stockwell, the dynasty's mean-spirited patriarch, has told some Texas-sized whoppers. But why should we spill his dirty little secrets when he's about to do it *himself?* Good thing the Stockwells have plenty of mansion insurance, because his confession could shake the shingles off this place!

Now brace yourself for this one! Caine's son, playboy tycoon Cord Stockwell, has just received some soul-shocking news. He's a *father*—and baby has come to Stockwell Mansion to roost. And by the fiery look in Cord's eyes, the sweet-'n-irresistible nanny he's temporarily hired might be staying for a *very* long time...say, until little Becky finishes college. Actually, *forever* sounds like a better idea, don't *you* think?

Cord's twin brother, Rafe Stockwell, wrangles with romance in *Seven Months and Counting...* SE #1375, available February 2001, only from Silhouette Special Edition.

Dear Reader,

Though each Special Edition novel is sprinkled with magic, you should know that the authors of your favorite romances are *not* magicians—they're women just like you.

"Romance is a refuge for me. It lifts my spirits." Sound familiar? That's Christine Rimmer's answer to why she reads—and writes—romance. Christine is the author of this month's *The Tycoon's Instant Daughter,* which launches our newest in-line continuity the STOCKWELLS OF TEXAS. Like you, she started out as a reader while she had a multifaceted career—actress, janitor, waitress, phone sales representative. "But I really wanted one job where I wouldn't have to work any other jobs," Christine recalls. Now, thirteen years and thirty-seven books later, Ms. Rimmer is an established voice in Special Edition.

Some other wonderful voices appear this month. Susan Mallery delivers *Unexpectedly Expecting!,* the latest in her LONE STAR CANYON series. Penny Richards's juicy series RUMOR HAS IT... continues with *Judging Justine.* It's love Italian-style with Tracy Sinclair's *Pretend Engagement,* an alluring romance set in Venice. The cat is out of the bag, so to speak, in Diana Whitney's *The Not-So-Secret Baby.* And young Trent Brody is hoping to see his *Beloved Bachelor Dad* happily married in Crystal Green's debut novel.

We aim to give you six novels every month that lift *your* spirits. Tell me what you like about Special Edition. What would you like to see more of in the line? Write to: Silhouette Books, 300 East 42nd St., 6th Floor, New York, NY 10017. I encourage you to be part of making your favorite line even better!

Best,

Karen Taylor Richman
Senior Editor

The Tycoon's Instant Daughter

CHRISTINE RIMMER

SPECIAL EDITION™

Published by Silhouette Books

America's Publisher of Contemporary Romance

For Gail Chasan, my favorite editor in the whole world, because she always senses when something's missing—and she never fixes what ain't broke.

Special thanks and acknowledgment to Christine Rimmer for her contribution to the STOCKWELLS OF TEXAS series.

 SILHOUETTE BOOKS

ISBN 0-373-24369-3

THE TYCOON'S INSTANT DAUGHTER

Visit Silhouette at www.eHarlequin.com

Printed in U.S.A.

Books by Christine Rimmer

CHRISTINE RIMMER

Since the publication of her first romance in 1987, *New York Times* bestselling author Christine Rimmer has written over thirty-five novels for Silhouette Books. A reader favorite, Christine has seen her stories consistently appear on the Waldenbooks and *USA Today* bestseller lists. She has won the *Romantic Times Magazine* Reviewer's Choice Award, and has been nominated twice for the Romance Writers of America's coveted RITA Award and four times for *Romantic Times Magazine*'s Series Storyteller of the Year. Christine lives in Oklahoma with her husband, younger son and two very contented cats, Tom and Ed.

Silhouette Special Edition is delighted to present

Stockwells of Texas

Available January—May 2001

Where family secrets, scandalous pasts and unexpected love wreak havoc on the lives of the infamous Stockwells of Texas!

THE TYCOON'S INSTANT DAUGHTER
Christine Rimmer
(SE #1369) on sale January 2001

SEVEN MONTHS AND COUNTING...
Myrna Temte
(SE #1375) on sale February 2001

HER UNFORGETTABLE FIANCÉ
Allison Leigh
(SE #1381) on sale March 2001

THE MILLIONAIRE AND THE MOM
Patricia Kay
(SE #1387) on sale April 2001

THE CATTLEMAN & THE VIRGIN HEIRESS
Jackie Merritt
(SE #1393) on sale May 2001

Available at your favorite retail outlet.

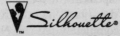

Visit Silhouette at www.eHarlequin.com

Chapter One

The social worker clutched the baby in her arms just a fraction tighter. "Mr. Stockwell, I'm sorry," she said. "But I can't leave Becky here under these conditions."

Cord Stockwell held on to his temper. "These conditions?" he repeated in his softest, most reasonable tone. Those who knew him best always had sense enough to proceed with care when he spoke so quietly. They knew that such a tone meant he wouldn't be speaking quietly for long. "Tell me. Exactly what is wrong with these conditions?" He lifted an eyebrow and waited, letting the big room around them speak for itself.

In the past five days, he'd had the room and the bedroom adjoining it completely redone. Now, rainbow murals arched across the sunny yellow walls. Brightly colored rugs dotted the hardwood floor. A rocking horse waited in the corner and big bins filled to the brim with toys were everywhere, along with an impressive array of stuffed animals. From teddy bears to baby dolls, the room had everything a little girl could ask for.

Cord added, still excruciatingly reasonable, "I went to considerable effort and expense to put all this together."

The social worker parsed out a pained little smile. "I can see that. And it's very nice. But—"

"But? I don't want any 'buts' out of you. I did every last thing you said I had to do—including hiring a nanny. Are you telling me it's *my* fault that the woman called this morning and said she wouldn't be able to take the job, after all?"

The pained smile got more so. "Of course it's not your fault. I never said it was. But the fact remains, you have no nanny. And in your particular situation, without appropriate child care, you aren't prepared to provide the kind of round-the-clock attention that Becky needs." The woman's tone, so preachy and know-it-all, would have done a Yankee proud. It thoroughly contradicted her down-home Reba McEntire twang. She'd grown up in some tiny town in Oklahoma; Cord would be willing to bet his considerable fortune on that.

He swore under his breath. An Okie social worker with a Yankee attitude. Did it get any worse?

Right then, the baby girl let out one of those little, gurgly cooing sounds that babies are always making. The social worker glanced down and met the baby's wide eyes—eyes the exact same shade of blue as the ones Cord saw when he looked in the mirror. The woman's tight expression loosened up. For a split second, as she smiled at the baby, she looked sweet and soft and pretty enough to make Cord forget how completely fed up he was with her.

Too bad a split second never lasts all that long.

She faced off against him once more, her mouth instantly pinching up tight as a noose around the neck of a hanged man. "A three-month-old baby is a full-time job. And you can't expect to be able to take care of Becky all on your own. As you explained to me yourself, you've got your hands full runnin' the Stockwell businesses, now that your father is ill. You're going to need help, and plenty of it."

Ill. Now there was a namby-pamby word for it if he ever heard one. Caine Stockwell was way beyond "ill." He was flat out dying. Of cancer. It was an ugly way to go. And Caine, mean as a stepped-on sidewinder in the best of times, was going down kicking and screaming all the way.

Cord tried again. "I told you. The Stockwell International offices are here, in Stockwell Mansion, right below us, on the first floor. I'll be available to Becky whenever she needs me. I'll find another nanny soon. And until I do, we've got help running out our ears around here anyway." Stockwell Mansion was a Dallas area landmark, the biggest house in the county of Grandview, forty Texas-size rooms in imposing Georgian style. It took a Texas-size staff to run the place. "One of the housekeepers can—"

"No, Mr. Stockwell," she interrupted him without so much as a by-your-leave. "One of the housekeepers can't. Becky deserves lovin', attentive care, not just someone willin' to look in on her now and then. And I intend—"

That did it. Cord's temper got away from him. "I don't give a good damn what you intend! That baby is—"

"—gonna start cryin' if you don't keep your voice down." Now the damn woman had her chin poked out. She was giving him her best Yankee-style glare. "And would you kindly stop your swearing, as well."

Fine. He would keep his voice down. He wouldn't

swear. Much. He suggested with measured care, "Listen. I want you to carry Becky into her bedroom, lay her down in her crib and then step across the hall with me."

She glared all the harder. "And why on earth would I want to go and do that?"

"So we can discuss this more…freely."

She made a snorting sound. "I don't think so, Mr. Stockwell. There is nothin' *to* discuss here." She had one of those big, flowered diaper bags hooked over her shoulder. She hoisted it higher. "I'll take Becky home now and when you've solved the nanny problem you can—"

"Just where the hell is this *home* you're taking my daughter to?"

She flinched, just barely, a reaction so small a less observant man would have missed it. But Cord Stockwell saw it, and took note of it. For the first time in their irritating association, he had gotten under Ms. Hannah Miller's skin. He wondered exactly what nerve he'd hit.

She tried to brazen it out. "Mr. Stockwell, as you very well know, paternity has not yet been medically established. Until the test results come back from the lab in San Diego, the state of Texas can't be completely certain that Becky is—"

"Come on. That's my baby, and we both know it."

Why me? Cord thought. Why of all the damn Child Protective Services workers in the giant state of Texas, did his baby girl have to draw this one? The woman was impossible. She had all the evidence she needed, for pity's sake. Marnie Lott, Becky's mother, who had died suddenly two weeks ago, had put Cord's name on Becky's birth certificate in the space reserved for the father. Why Marnie never bothered to let Cord know he was going to be a daddy was a mystery to him. But the dates matched. Cord's brief affair with Marnie had occurred almost exactly a year before—nine months prior to Becky's birth. And timing aside, all anyone had to do was look at her. If Becky wasn't a Stockwell, then neither was Cord.

Was Cord prepared for fatherhood? Hell, no. And he doubted that he'd ever be. But Becky was *his*. A Stockwell. Down the generations, the oil-rich Stockwells of Grandview, Texas, had been called hard-hearted, grasping, backstabbing and cold-blooded. But their worst enemies wouldn't argue on one point: a Stockwell took care of his own.

The social worker made a sniffing sound. "Maybe Becky is your daughter. Maybe she's not. The lab results will confirm or disprove your claim."

"My *claim?*" Cord grunted. "Let's cut through the bull here, Ms. Miller. That damn paternity test is no more than a formality. Becky's mine. And I will provide for her. I'll see that she has the best of everything. She'll go to the best schools. She'll never know what it is to do without. There are a lot of babies in this world who have a hell of lot less—nanny or no nanny. So it seems to me that the state of Texas ought to be just tickled pink over my *claim.*"

Of course, she had the classic comeback for that. "Money," she said, "is not all that a baby needs. A child also needs—"

He cut her off before she could get rolling. "Don't go there, Ms. Miller. Don't even get started in that direction. I've filled out your forms and answered your thousand and one way-too-personal questions. I've driven halfway across the county to meet you at that damn clinic so a nurse could stick a cotton swab in my mouth for the DNA test. I've set up the nursery you said I had to have. I've hired a nanny. She just never came to work. But it's not a big deal. As I've told you, I can manage without her until I replace her. Any other social worker would be more than satisfied that I'm ready and willing to be a father to my child. The question is, Ms. Miller, why aren't you?''

She gulped. The action gave him great satisfaction. Oh, yeah. He had her on the run now. "I've told you, I only want what's best for—''

"Didn't I ask if we could cut the bull? Let's get down to what's really going on here. Let's get down to how you plain don't like me.''

"I never said—''

"You didn't have to.''

"I—''

"You don't like me and you don't approve of me.''

"Well, uh, I—''

"I can see it in those eyes of yours. I can hear it in your voice. You've been reading the *National Tattler* and *Inside Scoop* magazine and you know what they say about me. I like women. I like them tall and I like them gorgeous—but I never like them for long.''

"I did not—''

"Sure you did. And that's okay. It's only the truth. And my reputation as a ladies' man has got nothing at all to do with the fact that that baby is mine and I will take care of her.''

Ms. Miller's face had flushed a burning red. "No. Now, you wait a minute. You wait just a minute. If you can't provide a stable, loving home for Becky, if you are gonna be out winin' and dinin' an endless string of women with whom you never intend to build a meaningful relationship, well, then, I do not see how I can bring myself to leave Becky in—''

"So I'm right.'' He gave her a slow, self-satisfied smile. "You don't approve of me—and you still haven't answered my first question.''

"Uh. What question was that?"

"Where are you taking my baby if and when you leave this house?"

She opened her mouth. And then she shut it. And then she gulped for the second time.

At last, with an embarrassed reluctance he found particularly pleasurable, she was forced to admit, "I'm licensed for foster care. Becky has been staying with me for the past several days."

It all made sense to Cord then. He allowed an agonized beat of silence to elapse before echoing quietly, "She's staying with you."

Hannah Miller drew her shoulders back and aimed her chin a notch higher. "Yes."

Cord couldn't help but gloat—just a little. "You know, I'll bet that doesn't leave a lot of time for your other cases. I mean, given that a three-month-old baby is—how did you put it? A *full-time job,* I think you said, a full-time job requiring *round-the-clock attention.*"

Those leaf-green eyes shifted away, but only briefly. Then she forced herself to look straight at him again. "I'm providin' what Becky needs. I had some vacation time coming and I took it. She is getting round-the-clock attention, I promise you that."

He delivered the telling blow, but he did it gently, in a softer voice than he'd used up till then. "Ms. Miller, you've let yourself get personally involved with my baby."

She blinked, her mouth went trembly. Cord enjoyed the sight more than he should have. "I...no. I—"

"The nanny isn't the issue here. The way I see it, the issue is twofold. You don't like me—and you don't want to let Becky go."

"No. I mean, *yes...*" She was really flustered now, her

cheeks flaming pink, her eyes wide and vulnerable. "I mean, whether or not I, personally, like you isn't the issue at all. And as for Becky, well, of course I love taking care of her. But I only want what's best for her. I only want—"

He moved a step closer, hiding his smile when she had to steel herself from shrinking back. And then he spoke, his voice low and gentle and utterly unyielding. "Take the baby into her room and put her in her crib. There's a monitor in there. Turn it on and bring the receiver back in here with you." He reached out. She stiffened. But then she saw what he meant to do. She actually aided him, shifting the baby to one arm for a moment, as he slid the strap of the diaper bag off her shoulder and set the thing on the floor. "Do it now," he added, even more softly than before.

For the first time in the twelve days he'd known the woman, she obeyed. She headed for the door a few feet away and vanished through it. A moment later, she reappeared—minus the baby, carrying the receiver.

He gave her a smile. She did not smile back.

"Now," he said. "Come with me."

Across the hall from the nursery, in his private sitting room, Cord gestured at a leather wing chair. "Have a seat."

Hannah Miller obeyed for the second time, perching right at the edge of the chair, tipping her head to the side a little, so she reminded him of a nervous bird, ready to take to the air at the slightest provocation. She still had the receiving half of the baby monitor clutched in her hand.

"Here." Cord took the device from her and set it on the marble-topped table at her elbow. "Relax. Drink?"

She frowned, then coughed, fisting her hand and placing it delicately against her mouth. "No. Thank you."

He shrugged. "Suit yourself."

At the liquor cart in the corner, he took his sweet time dropping ice cubes into a glass and pulling the crystal stopper out of a whiskey decanter. He poured himself a shot, reconsidered and splashed in enough to make it a double. Then he restoppered the decanter and looked at Ms. Miller again as he swirled the amber drink, ice cubes clinking in the process. He knocked back a sip. It warmed his throat, hot velvet, going down. Ms. Miller remained absolutely still on the edge of her chair, eyes wide and wounded, watching him—and waiting for whatever grim information he had to impart.

Cord sipped from his drink for a second time. The woman didn't fool him. She might look scared as a lost lamb at the moment—ever since he'd figured out she'd let herself get too attached to his little girl. But she was no lamb. She was a thoroughly exasperating creature who had made him jump through hoops to get what belonged to him. She was bossy and she wanted things done her way. Not his kind of woman at all.

But that shouldn't pose a problem. He didn't intend to date her or take her to bed. What he did intend to do was to see that his daughter got the best care available. And the woman showed a definite aptitude in that department.

"I've just come to a realization, Ms. Miller," he finally said.

She turned her head, but only enough so that she was facing him straight on. And she waited some more. He found he liked that: her silence, the fact that she didn't make some eager, hopeful little yes-person noise.

He said, "It occurred to me about a minute and a half ago that you and I want the same thing."

He paused—mostly to see if she'd lose her nerve and warble out, "What's that?"

She didn't. She went on waiting, looking apprehensive, but unbowed.

So he told her, "We both want what's best for Becky."

She opened her mouth a fraction—then closed it over whatever words she might have said. He knew, of course, what those words would have been. Something short. And skeptical: *Oh, really?* or *I doubt that.*

"It may come as a surprise to you," he said with ironic good humor, "but I want my daughter to have loving and devoted care every bit as much as you do."

She was looking at him sideways again. He supposed he couldn't blame her. Hell if he'd confess it, but he was pretty nervous about the whole idea of being a father. His own mother, Madelyn, had died when he and his twin, Rafe, were only four years old.

And his father was and always had been a coldhearted, verbally abusive SOB. It wasn't as if Cord—or Rafe, or their older brother, Jack, or their sister, Kate, for that matter—had known much in the "love and devotion" department when they were growing up.

But Becky could have better. Cord had seen it in the look on Hannah Miller's face when she stared down at his daughter. Becky would get all the love any child could ever want from a woman who gazed at her like that.

He swirled his ice cubes again—and made his offer. "Becky needs a nanny. And you don't want to let her go. So my question is, why should you? I'll pay you fifty thousand a year, plus the best benefits package Stockwell International has to offer, if you'll give up your job at Child Protective Services and come to work for me taking care of my daughter."

Chapter Two

Through a sheer effort of will, Hannah Waynette Miller kept her mouth from dropping wide-open.

She was stunned. Yep. That was the word for it. Stunned. Astonished. Astounded and amazed.

By Mr. Cord Stockwell, of all people.

He wanted *her* to be Becky's nanny?

She'd been sure the man disliked her. And she had told herself she didn't care. After all, she understood his kind. He was a rich man with a rich man's ingrained belief that the rest of the world existed for his comfort and convenience.

Well, Hannah Miller cared no more for what a man like that believed than she did for what he thought of her. Since that first day she had called him to tell him about Becky, she had never once put forth the slightest effort to make things comfortable for him—let alone convenient. For Becky's sake, she had stood her ground against him.

She had been determined to make sure that Becky got a real home, a home with love and attention and patience and hope in it. Of course, she always tried to make sure of those things for all of the children assigned to her care.

But she'd tried even harder with Becky. Too hard, maybe…

She hated to admit it, but the man had been right on that one little point.

She *was* much too attached to Becky, all out of proportion really, and she knew that. Hannah also knew she had to let go of the adorable blue-eyed darling and get on with her life. She had planned to do just that: to make certain Cord Stockwell found a loving nanny, one who would provide the intangibles that all his money could not buy. And then Hannah Miller had meant to be on her way—to return only if the paternity test she'd insisted he take proved he wasn't Becky's father, after all.

Cord Stockwell was waiting for an answer, standing there so tall and commanding on the other side of the beautifully appointed room, holding his glass of fine whiskey and looking at her with an amused expression on his too-handsome face.

Hannah knew what that answer should be: Thank you, but no. As much as she might wish it to be otherwise, as much as she had longed in the past seven lonely years for another chance, Becky was not her baby girl.

On the other hand, Hannah had no doubt that Becky did need her.

Cord Stockwell might be sexy as sin itself—he stood over six feet tall and he was possessed of lean hips, shoulders that went on for days and truly arresting deep blue eyes. An aura of excitement surrounded him. Even Hannah, who certainly ought to know better, couldn't help but feel the power of his presence every time she was forced to deal with him. And on top of the sex appeal and the charisma, he did have pots of money, money he was willing to lavish on Becky.

But did he know how to love and raise a sweet little girl? Hannah seriously doubted it.

Cord Stockwell sipped from his drink again. "Well?"

Right then, the telephone on one of the inlaid side tables buzzed.

Cord set his drink on the liquor cart. "Excuse me."

He strode to the phone, noting before he got there that it was his father's private line that had rung. He punched in the line and picked up. "What is it?"

"Mr. Stockwell, I'm sorry to bother you." It was a male voice with a slight Scandinavian accent, the voice of one of the nurses who attended his father round-the-clock—the big blond one named Gunderson. "But, sir, your father is insisting..."

In the background, Cord could hear the hoarse commands. "Get him in here. Get my boy in here. Now!"

The nurse reported the obvious. "He demands to see you, sir."

The cracked, rough voice shouted louder, "*Now,* I said. Are you deaf? Tell him to get in here on the double."

"I'm so sorry, sir." Nurse Gunderson made excuses in Cord's ear. "But right now, our problem is that he refuses to take his medication until you—"

"Get me Cord now!" the old man shouted.

A woman's voice—the other nurse—spoke up then. "No. Please put that down, Mr. Stock—"

Whatever it was, Caine must have thrown it. Cord heard what sounded like breaking glass.

The nurse on the other end of the line released a sigh. "Sir, maybe you should—"

"Try to keep him from hurting himself," Cord said.

"I'll be right there." Cord set the phone back in its cradle and started for the door. "Something's come up." He said as he strode past the wing chair where the social worker sat staring at him. "I'm afraid I have to deal with it now. I won't be long. You can think about my offer."

The door closed behind him before Hannah could say a word.

Cord could hear his father barking orders as he entered the old man's private sitting room.

"I don't need you poking me with needles. I can still swallow a damn pill if I need one. And right now, I don't need one. Not till I talk to my son, you hear me?"

One of the maids had joined Cord in the central hallway and followed him into the room. She carried a broom and a long-handled dustpan—probably under orders to clean up whatever mess Caine had created in his rage. The maid cringed when she heard the old man shouting.

"Don't worry," Cord said. "He's not yelling at you."

"Cord?" Cancer might be eating Caine Stockwell alive, but his hearing remained as acute as ever. "Cord, that you?"

Cord stepped through the wide arch that framed his father's oppressively opulent bedchamber—a replica, Caine always claimed, of Napoleon I's bedroom at the Château de Fontainebleau, the magnificent hunting lodge of sixteen and seventeenth century French royalty. The room, like the antechamber through which Cord had entered, boasted gilt medallions in classical motifs adorning the walls, a massive crystal and gold chandelier overhead and gilded furniture upholstered in carmine-and-green brocade. The huge velvet-draped bed, shipped from France a decade ago, was the room's crowning glory. And it stood empty. Caine would no longer trust the body that had betrayed him not to soil the dazzling stamped velvet bed coverings.

The room, in spite of its overbearing beauty, smelled musty and strangely sweet. Like sickness. Like encroaching death. The velvet curtains had been drawn closed against the hot Texas sun outside.

"Here. Here to me." Caine, who lay in a hospital bed in the center of the room, hit the mattress with one clawlike clenched fist, a gesture reminiscent of one summoning a dog.

Though Cord had always been his father's favored son, there had been a time when such a gesture would have had him turning on his heel and striding from the room, Caine's curses echoing in his ears. But that time had passed. In recent months, Cord had learned what pity was—and learning that had made it possible for him to put his considerable pride aside.

He approached the bed. Gunderson and the other nurse, a statuesque redhead, fell back to lurk near the rim of equipment—an oxygen tank, footed metal trays on wheels, an IV drip and the like—that waited several feet beyond where Caine Stockwell lay. The maid dropped to her knees and began picking up the pieces of a shattered antique vase, as well as a number of long-stemmed blood-red roses, which lay scattered across the gold-embroidered rug.

"Everyone out," Caine commanded. "You two." He flung out an emaciated arm at the nurses. "And you!" he shouted at the cowering maid.

Cord nodded at the others and instructed quietly, "Go ahead. I'll buzz you in a few minutes."

Caine's bed had been adjusted to a semisitting position. He lurched forward, as if he intended to leap upright and chase the others from the room. But then he only fell back with a groan. "Just get them out. Get them out now."

The three required no further encouragement. The maid jumped to her feet and scurried off, not even pausing to pick up her broom and dustpan, which lay where she'd dropped them, among the roses and broken china on the gold-embellished hand-stitched rug. The two nurses followed right behind.

Caine waited until he heard the outer door close. Then he patted the bed again, this time more gently. "Here," he said, his voice now a low rasp. "Here."

Cord did what his father wanted, taking a minute to lower the metal rail so there would be room for him.

"Have to tell you..." Caine coughed, a spongy, rheumy sound. "No more drugs. Until I tell you..." Caine coughed again. This time the cough brought on wheezing. "Got to tell..." He wheezed some more. "Have to say..."

Cord got up, but only to pour a glass of water. He brought it back to the bed, sat again and helped his father to drink, sliding a hand gently behind his head, feeling the heat and the dryness, the thin, wild wisps of hair. All white now, what was left of it. Once it had been the same deep almost-black color as Cord's hair was now. Dark, dark brown, and thick, with the same touch of gray at the temples.

But no more.

Caine's red-rimmed blue eyes glittered, sliding out of focus, vacant suddenly, shining—but empty. Cord carefully lowered the old man's head back to the pillow. Caine's eyelids drifted shut over those empty eyes. A ragged sigh escaped him, and a thread of saliva gleamed at the corner of his mouth.

Cord waited. In a minute, he'd rise, set the glass aside

and sit in one of the ridiculously beautiful gilded chairs to wait a little longer. Soon it would be time to ring for the nurses again.

Caine moaned. Cord sat still as a held breath, staring at the wasted specter that had once been his father. The old man had grown so weak the past few weeks. The skin of his face looked too tight, stretched thin across the bones. At his neck, though, it hung in dry wattles.

Cord glanced at his Rolex: 2:22. He'd give it five minutes and then—

His father's skeletal hand closed over his wrist, the grip surprising in its strength. "You listening?" The blue eyes blinked open. "You hear?"

Gently Cord peeled the bony fingers away. "I'm listening. Talk."

"More water."

Cord helped him to drink again. This time Caine drained the glass.

"Enough?"

"That's all."

Cord rose once more to put the glass on one of the metal trays. He came back to the bed and sat for the third time.

Dark brows, grown long and grizzled now, drew together across the bridge of the hawklike nose. "I lie here," Caine whispered, his voice like old paper, tearing. "Sleeping. Puking. Messing myself. I hate it. You know that?"

Cord said nothing. What was there to say?

"Sure, you know. You understand me." Caine laughed, a crackling sound, like twigs rubbing together in a sudden harsh wind. "You and me, cut from the same piece of high-quality rawhide..." The eyes drifted shut again and Caine coughed some more.

Then he lay still—but not for long. After a moment, he began tossing his head on the pillow, like a man trying to wake from a very bad dream. "I think about that baby," he muttered. "Lying here. Sick unto death. That baby haunts me."

Cord frowned. He must mean Becky.

For the last five or six years, Caine had taken to accusing his children, collectively and individually, of failing to do their part to extend the family line. So Cord had mentioned Becky to Caine about a week before, thinking it might ease the mind of the old tyrant to know he had at least one grandchild, after all. At the time, his father had only shrugged.

"You sure this baby is yours?" Caine had demanded. And when Cord had nodded, Caine had said, "Then it's a Stockwell. Bring it home. And raise it up right." And that had been the end of that conversation.

Apparently, though, Becky had stuck in Caine's confused mind. Maybe he wanted reassurance that Cord had done what needed doing.

"The baby's fine," Cord said. "She's here, right now. In her crib in the new nursery."

Caine sat bolt upright. "Here? *She's* here. A girl. It was a girl?"

"Yes," Cord said soothingly, guiding his father back down to the pillow. "A girl. Remember, I told you all about her? She's three months old. Her name is—"

"Three months! Do you think I'm an idiot? You think the cancer has left me no wits at all?" Caine sputtered and coughed. "It's almost thirty years now, since they left, that mealymouthed witch your mother and my turncoat twin. That baby's no baby anymore. It would be grown now. All grown up."

Cord suppressed a weary sigh. The red-rimmed blue

eyes were looking into the past now, through a very dark glass. Sometimes lately, the old man's mind rearranged the facts. Caine would imagine that his wife, Madelyn Johnson Stockwell, hadn't died in a boating accident on Stockwell Pond with Caine's twin, Brandon, after all. Caine would swear the two had run off together instead.

But this about the baby was new.

Caine fisted the sheets, his bony knuckles going white as the linen they crushed. Then he struck out, wildly, hitting Cord a glancing blow. The old man wore no rings. His fingers had shrunk too much; a ring would slide right off. But his yellowed nails needed trimming. One of them sliced a thin, stinging line along Cord's jaw. Cord pulled back sharply and touched the tiny wound. His finger came away dotted with crimson.

"It was mine," Caine ranted, his eyes closed now, the lids quivering, his head whipping back and forth against the pillow. "I tried. Tried to take care of it. Is it my fault she never would take the money?"

None of it made any sense to Cord. His mother and his uncle were long dead. And the only baby he knew about lay in a crib in another wing of the mansion, dreaming whatever a baby might dream of.

A baby.

His daughter.

The irony struck him. Someday, would he be the one ranting in a hospital bed, while his grown daughter sat patiently at his side?

It seemed impossible, that such a tiny, helpless creature as his baby girl would ever sit upright beside her father and watch as he died.

And why? Why would she perform such a grim duty anyway?

For love?

Cord almost smiled. He did not think it was love that he felt for *his* father. It was something darker, something more complex. Something with anger in it, and hurt—and maybe just a touch of reluctant respect.

No, he did not love Caine. But he did feel a duty to him, and he pitied him, pitied the bitter, half-crazed shadow of himself that Caine had become.

So he sat on the edge of his father's bed and let the old man flail his withered arms at him, striking him repeatedly, shouting more addled nonsense about Cord's long-dead mother and his uncle Brandon and a baby that Caine didn't seem to realize had never existed.

"Whatever your mother did, that baby was a Stockwell. Remember. We are Stockwells. We take care of our own. And I know her. She had a thousand reasons to hate me. But still, no matter what I said, I knew…deep down, I knew she was true to me. That baby…that baby was mine."

Cord took another series of sharp blows, to the shoulder, across the neck, to the center of his chest. By then, he decided it was time to buzz for the nurses.

His father needed calming. And Cord himself had to get back to his own quarters and finish up his negotiations with Becky's nanny-to-be.

After Cord left her, Hannah sat very still for several long moments.

What to do? How to answer?

Her heart's desire—to stay with Becky.

Her mind's wise instruction—to let Becky go. *Now,* though it would break her heart in two to do it.

She could get over a broken heart. She had done that more than once already in her twenty-five years of life.

But oh, if she lingered, it could only get worse. With

every day, every hour, every minute that passed, she would love Becky more. And the risk would be greater, the pain a thousand times more terrible, if for some reason, she had to let Becky go.

And that could happen, so very easily. Cord Stockwell was a rich man. And the rich—at least in Hannah's sad experience—*were* different. They broke rules. They broke hearts. They broke agreements. And they thought that their money gave them the right to run right over everyone else getting things their way.

Hannah sat up straighter.

Wait a minute, she thought. Just a cotton-pickin' minute here.

This was not seven years ago and she was a grown woman now, not some lost little orphan looking for love where she shouldn't be. And Cord Stockwell may have been too rich and too good-looking and too lucky with the ladies for her peace of mind, but he did seem, sincerely, to want to do right by Becky.

Her peace of mind was not the issue here. Neither was her foolish heart.

The issue was, what was right for Becky.

And she would make her decision based on that and that alone.

Right then, Hannah heard Becky cry. One short, insistent yelp came through the receiver on the table beside her.

A silence followed, but a brief one. In a moment, Becky started to wail. She was hungry.

Or she needed changing.

Or comforting.

Whatever.

Hannah rose to go to her.

* * *

Gunderson and the redheaded nurse reappeared a moment or two after Cord buzzed for them.

Cord was holding his father by then, an embrace that was actually an attempt to keep the sick man from harming himself. "More morphine," he said. "And it will have to be by injection. Get it ready. Now."

In his arms, Caine thrashed. "Didn't I? Didn't I keep my promise? Raised the bastard as my own…"

Gunderson glanced at his watch. "He had his last dose at—"

Caine raved right over him. "You witch…I loved you. Always loved you. All those others…nothing, damn it. Never. No one. Only you. But you…I know you loved *him*. Always. You never stopped. So I only wanted…to wipe out the taste of you."

Cord held his struggling father close and glared at the nurses. "Get it ready, I said."

The redhead filled the syringe. Cord held Caine still as she administered the dose.

Caine gasped. "Cold. Cold. Sinking…down…"

Within seconds, the old man went lax. Gently Cord laid him back against the pillow. A rank sigh escaped him and then he was still.

Cord rose from the bed. "Can you two take care of him now?"

"Of course, sir," said Gunderson.

The redhead nodded.

"Trim his fingernails, will you?" Cord commanded as he strode toward the door. "He cut me, they're so long."

Behind him, both nurses made sounds in the affirmative.

In the hall, he found the maid he had sent away earlier. She hovered near the door to his father's rooms, brown eyes huge with apprehension.

"It's all right," he said gently. "Go on in and finish up. He won't bother you. He's sleeping now."

The maid dipped her head. "*Sí.* Okay. Thank you, Mr. Cord."

He returned to his private sitting room to find that Hannah Miller wasn't there.

His first reaction was a hot burst of fury. The little upstart had dared to take his daughter and leave.

But then, over the baby monitor, he heard it: the soft sound of a woman's voice, sweet and only a little off-key, humming a lullaby.

He found her in the baby's bedroom, which had robin's-egg-blue walls, white furniture and a border near the ceiling of twinkling stars and smiling moons.

She sat in the white wicker rocker. She'd pulled up the shade of the window a few feet away to let in the afternoon light. She rocked slowly while she hummed, cradling his daughter and feeding her a bottle.

The woman's hair had both auburn and gold highlights, just slight hints of red and blond in the chestnut waves that fell to her shoulders. The curve of her cheek, as she bent over his daughter, looked pale as milk, soft as the petals of a white rose.

At first, she didn't see him. She had left the door open. And he entered quietly, listening as he came, for the soft sound of her lullaby, for the slight creaking of the rocking chair.

He stood there, in the doorway, watching the light on her hair, the curve of her arm as she cradled his child.

He felt the strangest sensation right then. A warmth down inside himself, a tiny bud of something.

It might have been hope.

But no.

More likely, it was only weary relief. The peace here, in his daughter's blue bedroom, was a thousand miles removed from the Napoleonic horror of his father's sickroom. And the little Okie's tongue could be sharp, but right now, she wasn't using it. Right now, she sounded damn sweet, humming and rocking away, a dreamy smile on her lips, as his child contentedly sucked at her bottle.

Naturally such a sight would soothe him, after what had just transpired in his father's room.

Hannah looked up. The humming stopped, the rocking chair stilled. He heard her quick, surprised intake of breath.

"Sorry," he said. "I didn't mean to startle you."

She shrugged. And then she actually granted him a smile. "This girl was hungry."

Damn. She was a pretty woman when she smiled.

He demanded, more gruffly than he intended to, "Have you made up your mind?"

She didn't seem bothered by his gruffness at all. She looked down at Becky again, said in a dreamy voice to match the expression on her face, "I have." She looked his way again, frowned. "You've cut yourself."

He touched the scratch on his jaw, where the beads of blood had dried now. "It's nothing."

"Don't rub it. You'll start it bleeding again—here." She produced a tissue from her sleeve and held it out. "Blot it real gentle."

He stared at the tissue dangling from her slender hand.

And, out of nowhere, an old memory popped to the surface of his mind and bobbed there, clear as a bubble made of glass.

Outside, in back, on the wide sweep of lawn between the house and the formal gardens. High summer. And ice cream. Vanilla with fudge syrup. He'd had a big bowl of it.

His mother had worn white—all white. Her blue eyes were shining and her dark brown hair tumbled in soft waves down her back. She had laughed. And she'd pulled a handkerchief from her white sleeve. "Cord, honey, you've got chocolate all over your little face. Come here to Mama. Let me clean you up...."

"Mr. Stockwell?" The social worker was staring at him, a crease of worry etching itself between her smooth chestnut brows. "Are you okay?"

"Yes," he said curtly. "I'm fine." He stepped up close and took the tissue from her, just to stop her from holding it out. And he blotted his jaw, as she'd told him to do. The tissue came away with two bright red spots on it. "There." He tipped it briefly toward her so she could see. "Nothing, as I told you."

She made a low, considering noise, as if she didn't agree, but could see no benefit in arguing the point.

He thought of his father, once so proud and strong, now weak and wasted, striking out, prone more and more frequently to episodes like the one today as death closed in on him. Maybe Ms. Miller was right. It meant a lot more than nothing, this tiny scratch on his jaw.

He tucked the tissue into the pocket of his slacks. "I'm still waiting for your answer." He couldn't resist adding, "You seem to enjoy that—making me wait."

He assumed she'd take offense. She was always so prickly. But no. She only smiled again, that smile that transformed her. "I'm sorry you think that. Of course, it's not even a tiny bit true."

"If you say so."

"I do."

"Fair enough."

Becky pulled away from the bottle then, and yawned wide and loudly. Cord watched his daughter, wondering how such a tiny mouth could stretch so big.

"Here." Ms. Miller tucked the empty bottle into the flowered bag on the other side of the rocker. "You can burp her." She found a cloth diaper in the bag and held it toward him, the same as she had that damn tissue a minute ago. "Put this on your shoulder. I'd hate to see you get spit-up on that beautiful shirt."

He scowled, thinking, *I'm Cord Stockwell. I don't do burping.*

"Take the diaper," she said.

So he took it.

"Put it on your shoulder."

He did that, too.

She gathered the baby close and rose from the rocker. Cord backed up.

"Come on," she dared to taunt him. "It's a skill you'll have to develop sooner or later."

"How about later?"

"How about now?"

What the hell choice did he have? He held out his arms and she put his baby in them.

"Good," she said. "Cradle her head. That's right. Now gently, onto the shoulder..."

Becky sighed when he lifted her and laid her against his chest. He could feel her little knees, pressing into him. She smelled of milk and baby lotion. And her hair was soft as the down on a day-old chick. She made a gurgling sound. And then she let out one hell of Texas-size burp.

"Excellent," intoned Ms. Miller.

He gave her a look over the dark fuzz on Becky's head. "I'm so relieved you approve—and are you coming to work for me, or not?"

She nodded. "I am. Temporarily."

He patted Becky's tiny back—gently. She was so small. It was like patting a kitten. "What does that mean, temporarily?"

"It means I'm going home now to pack up a few things and arrange for a neighbor to water my houseplants. Then I'll stay here, in the nanny's room, for a few days, or however long it takes to find you some quality live-in child care."

She would work for him. But not for long. Strange how he disliked the idea of her leaving. She was an exasperating female, but a damn worthy adversary, too. He could respect that. "Why don't you just take the job yourself? You're exactly the kind of nanny Becky needs. And I can guess what a social worker makes. Not near what I'm willing to pay."

Was that sadness he saw in those green eyes of hers? "Thanks for the offer, but no."

He stroked Becky's dark head and wanted to ask, "Why not?" But he held back the question. It was none of his business. And he doubted she would tell him anyway.

He inquired with ironic good humor, "I take it you're going to be interviewing nannies for my daughter."

"If that's all right with you, yes. I would like to do that."

"If that's all right with me? Ms. Miller, you sound downright agreeable."

"Enjoy it while it lasts, Mr. Stockwell."

"Ms. Miller, I intend to do just that."

Chapter Three

It was a little after seven that evening and Hannah was just putting the last of her clothes into the maple bureau of the nanny's room when the tap came on the door to the hall.

"It's open," she called.

A slim, dark-haired woman poked her head in. "Hi. I'm Kate. Cord's little sister—and Becky's aunt." Kate Stockwell smiled. She had a great smile. It lit up her fine-boned face. "You're Hannah, right?"

Hannah nodded. "Come on in."

"I'm not interrupting?"

"Nope. I just finished unpacking." Hannah turned to the bed, on which her ancient hard-sided suitcase lay open. With both hands, she levered it closed and pressed the latches. Then she grabbed the handle, lugged it to the floor and dragged it into the closet.

When she turned back to the room, Cord's sister was

standing near the bed. She was dressed for evening, her dark hair swept up, a little chain of diamonds dangling from each ear. Her dress was a simple cobalt-blue cocktail-length silk sheath that had probably cost a fortune at Neiman-Marcus. The dress brought out the blue of her eyes—eyes that watched Hannah with undisguised curiosity.

"Cord told me this afternoon that you'd be moving in for a while. You're not what I expected." Smoothing her dress beneath her, Kate Stockwell sat on the edge of the bed. "Then again, I'm not sure exactly *what* I expected."

Hannah frowned. "I don't understand."

"Well, I have to confess, Cord has mentioned you once or twice in the past several days. I mean, that you're Becky's caseworker with Child Protective Services. And that you're, um…"

Hannah did understand then. She laughed. "You are being so tactful. I think what you mean is that your brother didn't have too many nice things to say about me."

Kate's gaze slid away. "Well…"

Hannah said with cautious honesty, "Your brother and I don't always agree, I'm afraid. He's a very determined man."

Kate met Hannah's eyes again. "And you're pretty determined yourself, right?"

"That's about the size of it."

Kate was grinning now. "But you know, even if you two have had some disagreements, he seems pleased with the idea of your taking care of Becky."

"It's only for a few days—until I find the right nanny."

"Yes. I know. That's what Cord said."

Hannah still hovered by the closet door, feeling unsure. Her instincts told her that with this woman she could skip right on into "girlfriend" mode—but then that seemed inappropriate. She would no doubt be wiser to respect the usual professional boundaries between herself and a relative of one of her charges.

Kate looked confused. "What did I do?"

Hannah hesitated, still unsure how best to proceed.

And Kate caught on. "I get it. You don't know how to treat me—and I'll bet my brother's been giving you his Lord of the Manor routine. He does that. You'll get used to it. Underneath, he's a sweetheart, I swear to you. And the rest of us do our level best to act like normal human beings." She closed her eyes for a moment. "Well, I suppose I should clarify that. *Most* of the rest of us act like normal human beings."

Hannah wondered which Stockwell didn't fall in the "normal human being" category.

Kate didn't enlighten her. She sighed. "I'm rambling. But my point is, I meant it when I asked you to call me Kate."

Hannah looked into those blue eyes—so much like Becky's eyes, really—and decided to go ahead and follow her instincts. "All right. Kate, then." She left off hovering by the closet door to take the hand Cord's sister offered.

"And I don't have to call you Ms. Miller, do I?"

"Please. Just Hannah is great. You came to see Becky, I'll bet."

Kate nodded. "I can't believe it. Cord has a daughter. And I'm an aunt—but maybe she's sleeping. If she is, just tell me the best time and I'll come back."

"I put her down about an hour ago. We could go check on her—and just sneak back out if she's asleep. What do you say?"

Kate stood. "I'd love it."

Hannah led the way through the door that joined the

nanny's room to the play area of the nursery—and the darkened baby's bedroom beyond that.

Becky *was* asleep, lying on her back, her black lashes like tiny perfect fans against her plump cheeks. The two women stood over the crib. Hannah stared down at Becky, smiling like a fool, just grateful to be allowed to care for her for the brief few days to come. She heard a small sound from Kate—a sigh, she thought.

But when she glanced over at the other woman, what she saw made her want to cry out in sympathy. Such sadness. Such...despair, the eyes far away and lost, the soft mouth bleak and twisted.

Hannah couldn't stop herself. She reached out, touched Kate's slender arm. Kate shivered.

Hannah wanted to offer comfort—and to her, the greatest comfort in the world was cradling Becky against her heart. "Here. Hold her..." Hannah formed the words without giving them sound, already reaching for the sleeping child.

Kate caught her arm, mouthed, "Next time."

Hannah froze, mimed, "Are you sure?"

And Kate nodded, her delicate chin set. She gestured toward the door to the playroom, signaling that she was ready to go.

What else could Hannah do? She followed Kate out.

Back in the nanny's room, Kate said that she had to be on her way. "I'll be back, tomorrow, though, and see if I can catch that little darling awake." Her voice sounded brittle now, and way too bright.

"Tomorrow," Hannah promised, "we'll just wake her up if she's sleeping."

"Oh, no. She needs her sleep—and I'm sure you enjoy the break whenever she gives it to you. Tell you what, next time I'll buzz you first."

"Buzz me?"

Kate pointed at the phone on the nightstand. Hannah had been purposely avoiding confronting the thing, though the housekeeper, Mrs. Hightower, had briefly described its operation when she had ushered Hannah into the room an hour before. The darn thing looked as complicated as a switchboard.

"We all have our own private lines," Kate explained. "It's a big house and we can't go running from one end of it to the other every time we need to ask each other some simple little question. Cord is line two—that one buzzes both in his office downstairs and in his private rooms. I'm line four. And the new nursery is…" She craned toward the phone. "Ah. Cord's had it all set up. Thirteen."

Hannah pulled a face. "My lucky number."

"You'll get used to it."

"In the few days I'll be here? I doubt it."

"The outside lines are on the right. Just punch one of them if you want to make a regular call."

"Will do."

"I really have to go." A wry smile twisted Kate's mouth. "I'm due at one of those endless charity dinners. It is for a good cause, though. Raising money for learning-impaired children."

"See you tomorrow."

"It's a deal."

After Kate left, Hannah wondered about the bleakness in her eyes when she'd looked down at Becky dreaming in her crib. And beyond that, Cord's sister had gone and turned down the chance to hold the baby. Hannah couldn't understand how *anyone* could pass up an opportunity to have Becky in her arms.

Kate Stockwell had a secret or two, Hannah was certain

of it. And as a woman with a few sad secrets of her own, Hannah sympathized. In a sense, she did understand. In her heart. Where it counted.

Heck. Hannah *liked* Cord Stockwell's sister. And that was a pleasant surprise, given that Becky's supposed father was such a difficult man to get along with.

Cord ate his dinner alone in the sunroom. Kate had gone to some charity thing. Rafe, a Deputy U.S. Marshall, was on duty, transporting a federal prisoner to Washington, D.C. And their older brother, Jack—well, who knew where Jack might be? Like Cord, Rafe and Kate, Jack had his own rooms at Stockwell Mansion. But he rarely stayed in them. Jack lived all over the world, wherever new governments or old regimes were willing to pay for his highly skilled and lethal services.

After dinner, Cord went to his office in the West Wing. He'd only meant to wrap up a few things. But as usual, there was just too damn much that couldn't wait until tomorrow.

He worked into the evening. He had a number of contracts to review, correspondence to go over and a stack of business proposals that needed a decision from him yesterday.

The Stockwell empire had really begun with the oil boom of the thirties. Until then, Stockwells had been cattlemen, and not especially successful ones. It had been the land itself that had made them multimillionaires—or the black gold beneath the land, anyway.

For decades, the name Stockwell and the word "oil" had been almost synonymous. Stockwells drilled in and profited from oil fields from the Lone Star State to the Middle East.

When times got rough, they proceeded with care. And

during the boom years, they took chances. And they prospered.

In the eighties, when real estate became king again, Caine had seen the trend and jumped on it. And in the nineties, once Cord had graduated from UT and started working alongside his father, he had pushed even harder to diversify.

Now, when people heard the words, Stockwell International, they still thought "oil." But those in the know realized that the company had its fingers in a huge number of profit-making pies. Over the past few years, as he'd assumed more and more control, Cord had continued to channel investment capital wherever he saw potential. He backed shopping malls and high-tech companies just getting their start. And the projects in which he invested Stockwell capital almost always paid off and paid off well.

At a little after ten, Cord scrawled his name on the last in the stack of correspondence his secretary had prepared for him. Then he tossed the pen aside and ran his hand down his face. It was getting late. Time to call it a night.

Just then the phone on his desk rang—his private outside line. The caller ID window showed him a number he recognized. He hesitated before answering, thinking that he wanted to get back to his rooms, to check on his daughter—and on Ms. Miller, who by then should have been all settled in the nanny's room off the nursery.

The line buzzed again. He went ahead and picked up.

"This is Cord."

"As if I didn't know." The voice was soft. Extremely feminine. And thick with innuendo.

"Hello, Jerralyn." Cord leaned back in his chair.

Jerralyn Coulter was a Texas aristocrat—if there actually was such a thing. One of her great-great-great-great-grandfathers had perished at the Alamo. And her great-great-great-grandfather had been a true cattle baron. Cord and Jerralyn had been an item in the gossip columns for several weeks now. They'd hooked up at a political fund-raiser, a thousand-dollar-a-plate dinner where they'd been seated across from each other. It had started with smol-dering looks and teasing banter. He'd driven her home. And spent the night in her bed.

Jerralyn was twenty-six, an extremely beautiful and so-phisticated woman. Not to mention energetic. With a very naughty mind.

"Are you working late again?" she asked.

"Guilty."

"You work too hard."

"I like to work."

"You need to play—and I could be there in twenty minutes—with a bottle of Dom Pérignon in my hand and nothing on under my sables."

He laughed at that. "How can you wear sable? I thought you told me you were an animal rights activist."

"I was speaking figuratively."

"About the rights of animals?"

"No, about the sables."

"You are tempting," he said, still thinking of Becky, of the irritating Ms. Miller, of the way she hadn't seemed irritating at all, sitting in the white wicker rocker, her brown hair falling soft and thick along her cheek.

"And you are preoccupied." Jerralyn pretended to pout. "I could be hurt."

Cord blinked, rubbed his eyes. "Don't be. Later in the week?"

"Oh, all right. But at least turn the light off now and get out of that office. Workaholics are not sexy."

He promised her again that he was through for the night, and then said goodbye.

Emma Hightower, who had been the head housekeeper at Stockwell Mansion for well over a decade now, appeared in the doorway as Cord was turning off the lights. As always, she looked serious and sincere in her concern for his comfort. "Just making my last rounds. Is there anything else I can get for you tonight, Mr. Stockwell?"

"No, thank you, Emma. I'm fine. Did Ms. Miller get moved in all right?"

"Yes. She's all settled."

"You saw that she was fed?"

"I had dinner sent up to her room at seven-thirty, which seemed a good time for her, tonight anyway. By then, I assumed, she would have had sufficient opportunity to unpack her belongings. Consuela picked up the tray an hour later."

"And did Ms. Miller eat her vegetables?" he teased, hoping, as he'd hoped for years and years, to catch a hint of a grin on Emma's long, serious face.

"Yes," Emma said, serious as ever. "She seems to have a fine appetite."

"Good. It wouldn't do to have a picky eater for a nanny."

A slight crease appeared between Emma's thin brows, but she apparently decided that Cord's remark required no comment from her. She asked, "Would you like me to send a snack up for you tonight, Mr. Stockwell?"

"No, Emma. Thanks."

She went out and he followed, pausing to lock up the offices behind him. When he turned back to the wide hallway, Emma Hightower had disappeared.

Cord took the West stairway to the second floor, and his rooms, which were also in the West Wing, above the suite of offices. He passed up the door to his own bed-room, at the end of the wing, and proceeded straight to the room with the robin's-egg-blue walls, where his daughter should, by all rights, be asleep in her crib.

He paused before the closed door, listening—for a baby's cry, or possibly a woman's soft lullaby. But all he heard was silence.

Carefully, hardly realizing he was holding his breath, Cord turned the brass knob and slowly pushed open the door. The room was dark, the shades drawn against the moon outside. He tiptoed in, across the soft blue rug that in the daylight showed a pattern of swirling stars.

Yes. She was there. Sound asleep. He stood very still. After a minute, as the silence stretched out, he realized he could hear her breathing in tiny, even sighs.

As his eyes adjusted, he saw her more clearly, her round baby cheeks, her fat little mouth, that soft dark hair and the stubborn little chin.

All Stockwell. Yes.

He felt something tighten inside his chest.

All Stockwell.

Mine.

So strange. He'd never seen himself as a father. In all likelihood, he wasn't going to be a very good one. He worked hard and he played harder, and he left the joys of family for other men. He was too much like the old man who lay dying at the other end of the house, and he knew it, to be any good as a husband. Pity the poor woman who might have married him. He would have made her life a misery, because he'd betray a wife eventually. Monogamy just plain wasn't in him.

However, he'd always tried to be responsible, in his own way. He liked women. Plural. Well, not several at once. But a lot of them, one at a time. And while he was liking them, he'd always been damn careful not to get one of them pregnant. But apparently, with Marnie Lott—whose face, he felt a little ashamed to admit, he could hardly remember—he hadn't been quite careful enough.

And now there was Becky.

The more he got used to her, the more he looked at her and burped her and held her in his arms, the more he thought that having her was just fine.

Perfect, really.

He'd done his bit toward perpetuating the family line. And he hadn't had to get married and ruin some poor woman's life to do it.

Becky made a small, cooing sound. But she didn't wake. She cooed again, and rubbed her tiny lips together, then turned her head with a sigh toward the wall.

Cord stayed very still. He didn't want to wake her, really. She might start crying and then Ms. Miller would come flying in here, shooting him narrow-eyed looks—and then probably deciding it was time he learned to do more than burping. He'd end up changing a diaper or something equally unsettling. He knew that woman. And he understood the kinds of things she was going to start expecting him to do.

But Becky's eyes stayed shut. He watched the gentle rising and falling of her tiny chest and realized she wasn't going to wake up, after all.

He was just about to tiptoe out when he heard a faint sound—the creaking of a chair, perhaps, or the squeak of a floorboard. He looked up, through the open door to the playroom and beyond.

A sliver of golden light shown beneath the closed door to the nanny's room.

Ms. Miller was still awake.

Should that surprise him? It was only ten-thirty. No real reason she should necessarily have been sleeping.

Except, maybe, that he pictured her as someone who went to bed at twilight and rose before dawn.

He pictured her in a white cotton nightgown, with little bits of lace in small ruffled rows, at the cuffs and around the neck. The kind of nightgown a young girl would wear, so modest, covering everything—unless she just happened to stand in front of a lamp.

And then a man would be able to see it all: soft, secret curves sweetly outlined, and a tempting dark shadow in the V where her thighs joined...

Cord shook his head—hard.

What the hell? Was it possible he'd just had a sexual fantasy concerning Ms. Miller?

No. Not a fantasy. An erotic image, that was all. A quick flash on the screen of his overactive imagination, more proof of the unflagging persistence of his libido.

It meant nothing. He started to turn again.

But then he noticed the shadows. He could see them, moving across the floor. She was walking around in there.

Why?

Oh, for pity's sake, Stockwell, he thought in disgust. It's her room. She has a damn right to walk around in it whenever she wants.

But was she all right? Was something disturbing her? Was there something she needed, something he'd forgotten to make certain that she had?

She *was* his guest, after all, until she found her own replacement. At least, he supposed he should consider her a guest, since they'd never actually agreed on what he would pay her.

Now that he thought about it, what he would pay her was something they *needed* to agree on. He wouldn't take advantage of her. She didn't make a lot of money in the first place. She was also giving up her own vacation time to take care of his little girl and interview nannies for him. She deserved to be paid for it, and he intended to make certain she got what she deserved.

In several long strides, he covered the distance between his daughter's crib and the nanny's door. Leaving himself no opportunity to pause and reconsider, he knocked quickly, three sharp raps.

For a moment, after he knocked, there was silence. A thoroughly nerve-racking dead quiet. And then, at last, she pulled open the door.

Almost, he groaned.

He could not believe what his eyes were showing him.

Chapter Four

Cord looked down, to collect his scattered wits.

Her feet were bare. They were very nice feet. Pale and long, with pretty toes.

No polish. Uh-uh. No polish for Ms. Miller.

He couldn't resist. He let his gaze wander upward, taking in the white nightgown—white cotton, yes. Exactly. With the lamp behind her, he could see the outline of her ankles and the lower swell of a pair of surprisingly strong-looking calves.

But no more.

She hadn't followed his fantasy—correction, erotic image—to the letter, after all. She also wore a robe. A green one, of some indeterminate light fabric, over the white gown.

He imagined stepping forward and removing that robe.

But he didn't. He stayed right where he was—on the playroom side of her bedroom door.

Hannah clutched her nightgown at the neck and looked up into her employer's handsome face. "What is it, Mr. Stockwell?"

He cleared his throat. "Ms. Miller, we haven't discussed how much I'll be paying you."

She didn't understand his expression. It was a bewildered kind of look. And it didn't fit at all with the arrogant, take-charge kind of man she knew him to be.

"Um," she said, and swallowed. "Are you all right?"

His dark brows crunched up over that nose that belonged on a Roman coin. "All right? Of course, I'm all right. What do you mean?"

Now he looked angry. Oh, she did not like this. Something was happening here, and she didn't know what. "Well, it's just that you look so—"

"What?" He practically barked the word.

She backed up a step. "Nothing. Never mind." In an instinctive attempt at self-protection, she started to push the door shut.

He stuck out his right hand and stopped it. "I told you. I want to talk about your salary."

She looked at his outstretched arm, at his big hand gripping the door, and then she looked back at him. "Right now?"

"Why not?"

"It's eleven at night."

He lifted his free hand and glanced at the fancy watch on his wrist. "Ten forty-two."

"Will you please let go of the door?"

He did. She considered shutting it in his face. But she couldn't quite bring herself to do it. She kept thinking how lost he'd looked a moment ago, and, well, feeling just a tiny bit sympathetic toward him.

Which was crazy. Cord Stockwell did not require her sympathy.

But still, she didn't shut the door on him. She only stood there, her fingers nervously stroking the small lace ruffle at the neck of her nightgown.

All right, she thought. He wants to talk money. We'll talk money. We can do that quickly. And then he can go. "Well, um. As I told you before, I'm on vacation anyway. So it isn't really necessary for you to—"

He swore. "Don't give me that. I hired you to do a job. You will be paid for it."

"It's only for a few—"

"Just name a price."

"Okay. Fine. How about a daily rate?"

"Good. Whatever." He kept staring at her neck, where her hand fiddled with the lace. She made herself lower that hand, and then felt too exposed to simply drop it to her side. So she wrapped both arms around her middle and came up with a figure.

"I'd pay more," he said.

"You said to name a price. I did. Accept it."

"Well. If you're sure…"

"I'm sure. We can settle up when I leave."

"All right, then," he said with finality.

But then he just stood there.

And so did she.

After what seemed like a year, he asked, "So. You're all right? Comfortable? Got everything you need?"

"Yes. The room is very nice. I have no complaints at all."

"Good."

More silence. She found herself studying the strong line of his jaw, noticing, in the wash of light from the floor lamp behind her, that there were strands of silver in his dark hair—only a little, at the temples. It gave him a rather distinguished look. He was wearing the same dress shirt he'd worn that afternoon, a beautiful blue one. It had a lovely rich luster. He also wore dark slacks.

The clothes fit him perfectly. He probably had a tailor who made them especially for him. He would require custom fitting, for those wide shoulders and powerful arms— and that deep, strong chest that tapered down to a tight, hard waist.

They were staring at each other. And they'd been doing it for too long.

He seemed to shake himself. "It just occurred to me…"

"Yes?"

"Feel free to use my sitting room across the hall for the interviews."

"Thank you." Her own voice pleased her mightily right then. She sounded so self-possessed. "I will use the room, if we need a place to sit down and talk."

"Good then," he said. And was quiet again.

Suddenly he seemed to realize that he couldn't just stand there, staring at her for the rest of the night, waiting for some other piece of information to occur to him.

"Well. I suppose I should let you get back to… whatever it was you were doing," he said.

She couldn't help grinning. He actually was rather appealing like this, kind of confused and strangely dear. She heard herself volunteer, "I was just pacing the floor, thinking up my list of qualifications for the new nanny. I'm going to put an ad in the paper and try a few of the best employment agencies. So far, I've come up with, 'Dependable, loving and live-in…' Any suggestions?"

He smiled back at her. Oh, the man could smile. No

wonder he had women dropping like flies. "How about 'Experienced?'"

"Good one."

"And 'References Required.'"

"Oh, absolutely. I got that. I did. And I wanted to ask you, what about salary? And maybe I should know a little more about the benefits package you offer."

He quoted a very generous figure. "As to benefits— full medical, and we have a dental plan. And an optical plan, as well. All the major holidays—or time and a half if she agrees to work a holiday. And two weeks vacation a year."

Hannah could see that she'd have no trouble at all filling this job—good money, fine benefits and the chance to watch Becky take her first step, sound out her first word, learn to ride a bike...

What more could any woman ask for? If she didn't watch herself, she'd end up pea-green with envy of the woman she was planning to hire.

"Anything else?" he asked. He looked kind of hopeful. And for some reason that made her want to try to think up more questions.

But how wise would that be?

"Um. No. I think that's everything. Thank you."

"You're welcome." He kept smiling that killer smile. But after a minute it faded.

He finally said, "All right. Good night."

"Yes. Good—"

They both heard the cry at the same time—well, it was more of a whine, really. A small, fussy, tender little sound. They stared at each other. Hannah was holding her breath.

And she knew that he was, too.

Another whine. And then a louder one. And then an outright cry.

Hannah told him ruefully, "Someone is calling me." She moved forward a fraction, and then hesitated. "Excuse me."

"Oh. Sorry." He stepped back, out of the doorway.

She brushed past him.

Cord just stood there, staring after her as her bare feet whispered across the playroom floor, the bit of snowy-white nightgown that showed beneath her robe seeming to glow in the darkness as she retreated. When she disappeared through the door to the baby's bedroom, he bestirred himself and followed.

She was lifting Becky from the crib as he reached her side.

"She might be wet. And she's probably hungry. I usually feed her around eleven. And she's a good girl." She cooed something appreciative into Becky's tiny ear, then added, over the baby's shoulder, "After this, she'll most likely sleep through the rest of the night."

She turned for the white bureau nearby, the one with the changing pad on top. He had a feeling what was coming. And it was.

She laid the squalling baby on her back, then slid a finger down her diaper. "Yep. Time for a change."

He considered backing up until he was out the door. But unfortunately, she spoke before he could get his legs to move.

"Come on." She flicked on the little carousel wall lamp next to the bureau. "You need to learn how to do this. And it won't be so tough. It's only wet this time." She had the nerve to grin at him.

"Maybe I should wait," he suggested, wincing as his little girl squalled, flailing her arms and kicking her fat little legs. "I'll give it a try sometime when she's not squirming so much."

"Mr. Stockwell, babies who need changing most generally are going to squirm."

"See. There you have it."

"Have what?"

Becky, who didn't look nearly as cute right then as she had when she was sound asleep, kept on yowling and waving her arms and legs around. She was wearing some little yellow T-shirt thing with snaps all over the front of it.

Ms. Miller made more cooing sounds as she peeled away tabs.

"You should do it," he said. "You're good at it."

"And you should learn. Come on over here."

Hell.

He took the few steps to stand by the changing pad with her. She already had the diaper off. She pressed a lever with her foot, and tossed it into the white bin beside the bureau. Next, she reached over and pulled a couple of white squares out of a plastic container.

She held out the squares. "Here. These are baby wipes. Take them."

He should have known better, but he did what she told him. The damn things were *wet*, for the love of Mike. His disgust must have shown on his face.

Ms. Miller let out a loud hoot of laughter.

Surprised the hell out of him—and Becky, too. His little girl stopped yowling to stare at the woman standing over her.

Ms. Miller had the grace to shut her mouth. "Oops," she said. "Sorry." She looked away—to control herself, presumably. He heard one more snicker and then she turned back to him with a straight face.

He was still holding the wet squares from the plastic container.

Ms. Miller said, "Wipe her bottom. Very gently."

He said nothing, only shook his head and stepped closer and did what she said that he had to do.

Once that was accomplished, she had him throw away the used wipes. Then she handed him the diaper rash ointment and told him to gently rub it on. And then, she showed him how to fold a diaper into the slots on the pair of plastic pants. Finally she had him take Becky's little feet and lift up her bottom and slide the diaper and plastic pants underneath her.

After that, it was pretty simple. He folded the sides up and pressed the Velcro tapes together.

"Now," she said, "we'll wrap her back up nice and cozy in this light blanket and you can hold her for a few minutes. I'll stick a bottle in warm water. Be back in a flash."

She was gone before he could order her to stay. A dim light went on somewhere in the playroom.

How long did it take to warm up a bottle?

Too long, more than likely.

Becky looked like she might just start crying again. So he picked her up very carefully and put her on his shoulder the way Ms. Miller had shown him before. And then he stood there, feeling like ten kinds of oafish idiot, patting her little back and listening to Ms. Miller in the other room, bustling around in there, doing whatever had to be done to get Becky's nighttime snack ready.

Becky made a little, experimental sort of fussy sound.

He did not want her starting to yowl in his ear. Maybe if he rocked her...

Yes. That would be good. Babies liked rocking. Didn't they?

He carried her to the rocker and carefully lowered the two of them into it. He rocked very gently, thinking that would be more soothing, though he felt just frantic enough to keep having to remind himself not to pick up speed.

Becky whined. And then she cried. She also burped. He felt that. It was a wet burp and it made a warm, soggy spot on his shirt. That was when he remembered that he should have put a diaper on his shoulder before holding a baby there.

He went on rocking.

Becky went on crying.

And finally, Ms. Miller reappeared with a bottle.

He didn't know whether to hug her or yell at her.

She went to the rows of shelves over the changing area and got the diaper that he'd forgotten to use. And then, finally, she padded over to him on her pretty white feet. She set the bottle on the little table by the rocker.

"Here," she said, calm and competence personified. Gently she peeled Becky off his shoulder.

He looked up at her. "What now?"

"Now you can feed her."

He started to argue, just on principle. But then he thought that feeding her might not be near as bad as rocking her while she wailed. She'd have a bottle in her mouth, right? And that meant she'd be quiet.

So he allowed Ms. Miller to lay his daughter in his arms, then to hand him the bottle. The rest was easy. He touched the nipple to Becky's mouth and she latched on and started sucking away.

Piece of cake.

He grinned down at her, pleased with himself, pleased with Becky—and also pleased, though he probably shouldn't have allowed himself to be, with Ms. Miller.

"You've got drool on that nice blue shirt," Ms. Miller said softly.

He smiled down at his gorgeous, hungry daughter. "Breaks of the game."

"Here." She bent close. She smelled warm and sweet, of woman and baby lotion and some faint, light perfume. She smoothed the diaper on his shoulder. He didn't even realize he'd stopped rocking until she pulled away and he lost the scent of her. Slowly, cautiously, he started the chair moving back and forth again.

"When she's done, burp her—you remember how to do that?"

He didn't look up. It seemed safer that way.

She continued, "Then put her in the crib again. On her back. Tuck her in nice and cozy. You think you can handle that?"

He wanted to say, "Maybe not. Maybe you'd better stay…" But where the hell would that get them? She was a smart-mouthed, well-meaning social services worker from Anywhere, Oklahoma. The kind who married, settled down with one guy forever and raised a passel of kids. And he was a man with no interest in anything that had settling down in it—let alone forever.

All right. He'd admit it. She held a certain…attraction for him. He didn't understand it, because he never dated the homey, settling-down type. Not ever. And he never went after the help. It was a cardinal rule with him.

He didn't understand it.

But did he even need to understand it?

He realized he didn't, since he knew it would pass. His interest in any one woman always did. It would be the same with Ms. Miller—except that, in her case, he would never lay a hand on her. She'd teach him the things he needed to know about taking care of his little girl. And she'd find her own replacement, someone steady and dependable, someone minus the leaf-green eyes and the chestnut hair, the shapely feet and the virginal but see-through white nightgown.

"Mr. Stockwell, can you handle it?"

He looked up at her then. "Where were you born, Ms. Miller?"

She hesitated, but then she did tell him. "Oologah. That's in—"

"I know where Oologah is. Birthplace of Will Rogers. Have I got it right?" She nodded. He asked, "What did your daddy do?"

Another hesitation. Then a sigh. "He ran a gas station. I was pretty little, but I still remember those gasoline trucks pulling into our station to fill up the tanks. They had your name on the side of them. Stockwell Oil."

"Your folks still live there, in Oologah?"

Something happened in her face, a barrier descending behind those green eyes. "No, Mr. Stockwell. They do not. And you haven't answered my question. Do you think you can put Becky to bed by yourself?"

"Yes, Ms. Miller. I believe that I can."

"The monitor's on the windowsill. I've got the receiver in my room. Just speak up if you need me."

He held her gaze for much longer than necessary before he answered, "Thanks. But I'm sure I can manage just fine on my own."

She turned for the door. He glanced down at Becky. Looking at his daughter kept him from watching the bit of white gown that fell below the hem of her robe, and the outline of Ms. Miller's calves beneath it, not to mention the unconscious invitation in her gently swaying hips as she walked away from him.

Chapter Five

Kate Stockwell called Hannah on the house line at eight the next morning. "Is she awake? I thought I'd stop in before I go down to breakfast."

Hannah smiled. "Yes, she is."

Not five minutes later, Kate breezed into the nursery. "Okay, I'm here. Do I get to hold her?"

Hannah passed the baby over, and Kate gathered her close. Whatever shadows Hannah had seen in those deep blue eyes the evening before had been banished, apparently, with the new day.

Kate sat in the rocker and cooed to her niece. She was wearing a silk pantsuit that must have cost more than Hannah brought home in a month. However, like her brother, Kate didn't seem to care in the least if Becky drooled all over her designer duds.

Eventually Kate spared a glance for Hannah. "Interviewing for your replacement today?"

Hannah lifted a shoulder in a half shrug. "Maybe. I should at least get the ads in the papers and call the agencies. The agencies might manage to get some applicants over here today—and they definitely will by tomorrow. I'm expecting this to go real quickly. In a few days, the new nanny will start work and I'll be out of here."

Kate grinned. "You said that yesterday. Are you trying to convince me...or yourself?"

"Just stating the facts."

Kate wasn't buying. "Don't think you can fool me, Hannah Miller. I spend my workday digging out what's going on beneath the surface. You love this baby. You don't want to leave her. Ever."

What could Hannah say? "You're right. I love Becky. And the last thing I want is to leave her. But I will. And very soon."

"Cord told me he asked you to take the job yourself."

"Yes, he did."

"So why won't you?"

"It's best that I go."

"Is it?"

Hannah let that question stand as rhetorical and back-tracked to a safer subject. "You said you spend your day 'digging out what's going on beneath the surface'? You're a therapist."

"How did you guess?"

"I didn't. Your brother mentioned what you do, in one of our first interviews. I asked for background on the other adults who might be a part of Becky's life."

"Ah. Well, I'm an art therapist, to be specific. I work with troubled children."

"Your patients draw and paint for you?"

"And sometimes we work with clay. Or with mixed

media. You name it, I'll use it…if it works to help me reach them.''

"I can tell by the way you talk about it, you like your work."

"I love it." Kate stood from the rocker, cradling Becky close against her silk-covered shoulder as she did it. "Oh, she feels like heaven in my arms. I can't believe she'll be right here from now on for me to cuddle and fuss over whenever I feel like it."

"Believe it. She's not going anywhere."

Kate shot Hannah another loaded glance. "*Unless* that paternity test you made my brother take shows he's not Becky's daddy, after all."

The paternity test. Oh, Lord. She had almost forgotten about that. "Well. Yes. If the test shows that your brother isn't Becky's father, it *could* make a difference."

Kate kissed Becky's temple and nuzzled her ear, then turned that blue gaze Hannah's way again. "I can't believe you got him to take that test in the first place. The way I understand it, with the evidence you had pointing to Cord as the father, and considering that there was no one contesting his claim, no paternity test should have been required."

Hannah looked away. The shades were up, providing a view of sweet gum trees and oaks and a section of lawn. Lord, there was a lot of lawn out there. It must cost a fortune to keep it green during a scorching Texas summer—which this one was already stacking up to be. In the distance, Hannah could see the driveway that wound toward the road.

"Hannah," Kate chided. "If you're unwilling to talk about this, just say so."

Hannah made herself meet the gaze of the woman she had already started to think of as a friend. "You're right.

I insisted on the test, though in this particular case, the State of Texas didn't require it."

"But how in the world did you manage to get Cord to take it?"

"I said that if he *didn't* take it, there would always be a doubt."

The two women regarded each other over the fuzzy dark curls on Becky's head.

"Very clever," Kate said.

Hannah crossed her arms over her midsection. "As soon as I brought up the issue of doubt, he *had* to take that test. That's the kind of man he is."

"You know my brother very well."

Hannah wasn't sure she liked the sound of that. "No, I don't. I don't know him at all. I just know he likes to run things. He likes to…be on top. He's a leader. And part of being a leader is wanting to know where you stand. If Becky is proven, beyond a shadow of a doubt, to be his, then he'll never have to worry about the possibility that someone else might make a stronger claim on her later."

Kate said softly, "I'm thinking that there's someone right now, someone who'd like to make a claim of her own. And I'm thinking that someone is you. Am I right?"

Hannah didn't answer, but Kate must have seen the truth in her eyes.

"I knew it." Kate kissed Becky's soft cheek. "And I can't say I blame you—but you'll be disappointed, I'm afraid. This is Cord's baby. Anyone could see it."

"I just want her to be happy. I want her to have a good life. In every way."

"We will take good care of her. If my brother hasn't promised you, then I'm promising you now. And being an aunt is very important to me. I...don't have any children of my own.''

Hannah hastened to make the proper reassuring noises. "Oh, but I'm sure you will. Someday.''

Kate only shrugged. "Here. You'd better take her. I've got my first appointment at nine. Got to get going...''

Hannah took the baby, and Kate turned to go.

But then Cord appeared in the door to the hall, dressed for a day of wheeling and dealing in an absolutely gorgeous gray three-button suit, the fabric of which looked lightweight enough to be comfortable even in a Texas heat wave.

"Kate,'' he said, looking pleased to see his sister there.

She fondly touched the side of his face. "Hannah let me hold her. I adore her. We'll have to watch out or we'll end up spoiling her rotten.''

He chuckled, the sound low and warm. "Watching out won't help. We'll spoil her anyway. We won't be able to stop ourselves.''

"We'd better.'' Kate faked a man's deep, rough tone. "Nothin' worse than a damn spoiled brat.''

Both sets of blue eyes turned somber.

Kate said, "Do you think we ought to take her in, to see him?''

Cord gave one quick shake of his head. "I told you how he was yesterday. Completely out of his mind.''

Kate said, "I stopped in to see him about six.''

"And?''

"He was sleeping.''

"He's on so many meds, he's either agitated as hell— or dead to the world.''

Kate sighed. "Yes, I guess so.''

Cord said, "I just don't know if I'd feel right about bringing Becky into that room.''

"Has he asked to see her?"

"No."

"Then forget I made the suggestion. Let's not even consider it, unless he specifically asks for her." Kate edged around her brother. "Gotta run." She sent a wave over her shoulder. "I'll be back, Hannah."

Hannah waved in return. "Anytime." And then Kate was gone.

Cord, however, was going nowhere. He shrugged out of his beautiful jacket, making Hannah more than a little uncomfortable because he watched her like a hawk while he did it. "My father," he muttered, as if that explained everything.

And it did, to a degree. "Yesterday afternoon," she said. "When you had to leave so suddenly…"

"Right. I've told him about Becky. But he's…very confused. He's on a number of medications for his illness, including heavy-duty painkillers. I'd like to take her to him, to let him see he has a granddaughter. But his behavior can be scary. Erratic. He can be violent. Both physically and verbally. He was never a particularly kind man. But recently…" He let the grim sentence finish itself.

Hannah found herself aching for both him and Kate, to have to watch their father die such an ugly, painful death. "I'm so sorry."

He acknowledged her expression of sympathy with a nod, and then forced a lighter tone. "You and my little sister seem to get along just fine."

Hannah caught Becky's tiny hand and kissed it. "I do like Kate. She's fun and smart and down-to-earth."

"Not a hopeless, overbearing snob like some of us Stockwells." He tossed his jacket over a straight chair by the door and strode toward her.

She was aware of a certain strange fluttering feeling in

her stomach, which she told herself to ignore. "I never said you were a hopeless, overbearing snob."

"But you thought it." He reached for Becky.

Hannah passed the little darling over. "I did not." Well, all right. It was a lie, but for a good cause. She added, "And you need a diaper on your shoulder, pronto."

"So give me yours."

She did, smoothing it in place, trying to ignore the fresh-showered scent of him, which was equal parts man and a wonderful, subtle no doubt expensive aftershave. He looked past Becky and right into her eyes. The butterflies in her stomach went wild.

Hannah stepped back, though she couldn't quite bring herself to break the hold of his gaze. They stared at each other. And then Becky made one of those darling, gurgling sounds.

Cord blinked. And so did she.

And everything was normal again.

More or less.

He asked, "So what's on the agenda for today?"

She told him what she'd told Kate—that she'd contact the newspapers and the agencies, maybe even conduct an interview or two in the afternoon. "And this morning, while it's still reasonably cool, I thought I'd get out that fancy new stroller I found in the closet and take Becky for a walk. It looks like miles and miles of grass out there, and plenty of shade trees. I'll bring her in before it gets too hot. Would that be all right with you?"

"Sure. What time?"

Hannah frowned at him. Did it matter exactly what time she went?

He answered the question she hadn't asked aloud. "I'll go with you...if that's all right?"

She stared at him, thinking, *is* it all right? There was no reason why it shouldn't be.

Except...well, she hadn't really anticipated seeing very much of him in the few days it would take her to find him proper child care. She'd thought he might drop into the nursery now and then. But it hadn't occurred to her that he might want to go with her and Becky for things like walks outside.

Then again, if that paternity test turned out the way everyone seemed to think it would, Becky would most certainly spend her childhood here, in this big suite of rooms at Stockwell Mansion. And Hannah would have been remiss in her duty if she didn't encourage Becky's father to spend every moment he could with her.

"Well?" He was giving her one of those raised-eyebrow looks of his.

She forced a bright smile. "Yes. Of course, you're welcome to walk with us. I just thought...that is, I understand you work very hard."

"I do. And I make my own schedule. If I want to take off an hour now and then, I do. That's one of the good things about being the boss."

"Well, okay then. Say, eleven o'clock?"

"Eleven is good." He carried Becky to the changing table, laid her down and picked up a rattle from the shelf above. He shook it. Becky blinked her blue eyes and let out a giggle.

"She's a happy girl," he said, and shook the rattle some more. He looked up and snared Hannah's gaze. "I could feed her..."

Those butterflies in her stomach grew agitated again.

Not good, Hannah thought. Inside her head, her own voice cautioned, Whoa, girl. Watch yourself....

A frown pleated his forehead. "Are you all right?"

"Oh, yes. Fine. Why?"

"You seem distracted this morning."

"No, I'm not distracted. If Becky were hungry, we would know it."

He spoke to his daughter. "Hear that? Ms. Miller says you're not hungry. That so?"

He shook the rattle, and Becky loosed another peal of baby laughter.

"I'll take that as a yes." He bent closer. And then he put his lips against the little bit of plump belly that showed between the lacy baby shirt and the matching pink bottoms that went with it. He blew a long, loud raspberry.

Becky crowed in delight.

And something inside Hannah went to mush.

Luckily Cord Stockwell didn't look up. He went on shaking the rattle and talking to Becky, calling her beautiful, asking her if she'd had a good night's sleep and pretending she was answering him when she chortled and waved her arms and legs and made those silly, drooly, goo-gooing sounds.

It was a perfect opportunity to leave them alone for a few minutes of high quality father-daughter bonding—not to mention a chance to escape and pull herself back together, get those mushy feelings under control.

"Um. If you're going to be here for a few minutes, I'll—"

He glanced up. "You're leaving us alone?"

The anxious expression on his face had her hiding a grin. "You know I'm only two rooms away. Just call if you need me."

"Wait a minute. She's not about to require a serious diaper change, is she?"

"Serious?"

"Yeah. Serious. Beyond just wet. I think I'm okay with

wet now. But for anything more, I'm going to need some assistance.''

"I see."

"What is that look you're giving me, Ms. Miller?"

"Mr. Stockwell, I am not giving you a look."

"You'd better not be. I'm a man who needs help with a loaded diaper and I'm not one damn bit ashamed to admit it. Are we clear on that?"

"Well, yes. I'd say we are."

"Good."

"I don't think you have anything to worry about right now. She had a *serious* diaper change about a half an hour ago."

"Well, why didn't you say so? Go ahead, then. Take a break. Did you get breakfast?"

"Not yet. Mrs. Hightower said I should buzz the kitchen when I was ready for it. I'll do that now."

He made a sound in the affirmative, but he was already bent over Becky again.

In her own room, Hannah kicked off her soft-soled shoes and called the kitchen. She asked for a poached egg, whole-wheat toast, tomato juice and coffee with cream. The woman who took her order said Hannah would have the food within twenty minutes. Hannah thanked her, marveling at the whole idea of a house so big you could order your breakfast by telephone, like takeout from a coffee shop.

Then she used an outside line to call the papers to place the ads she had written up the night before. That went quite smoothly. It took ten minutes to get things set up with the *Morning News.* And even less than that for the *Grandview Gazette.*

Courtesy of the baby monitor perched on her windowsill, Hannah kept hearing the sounds from the other room: Cord's deep, teasing voice, talking to his daughter. And Becky's baby noises that seemed almost like replies.

Cord's voice grew softer. It actually sounded as if he were telling Becky a story. Hannah caught an occasional phrase: "The first Caine Stockwell...a rancher, and not very good at it. And Noah, my grandfather. He built this house..."

A family history. Hannah couldn't help smiling. Evidently, three-month-old Becky was getting an early start at understanding what it meant to be a Stockwell.

"Excuse me," said the ad sales rep from the *Morning News*. "That was 'dependable...'"

"Yes. And 'loving...'" Hannah ordered herself to tune out the deep voice in the other room and concentrate on getting the ad right.

The knock at the hall door came not thirty seconds after she'd completed the second call. She got up and let the maid in.

"Just set it down there. Thanks."

The maid put the tray on the little desk by the window and quickly took her leave. Hannah poured coffee from the insulated pot into the pretty china cup, added cream and sipped, wondering if she ought to go ahead and eat— or if Cord would be calling for her soon, ready to be on his way.

The monitor on the windowsill was quiet now. Maybe—

Right then, there was a soft tap on the door to the playroom.

Hannah carried her cup with her to answer.

He was waiting on the other side of it, his jacket across his arm—and no Becky in sight.

Cord put a finger to his lips. "I was telling her all about the oil embargo of the seventies. She seemed fascinated.

But then, all at once, I realized she was only quiet because she was asleep. I almost woke her up to tell her that a little girl should never go to sleep when her daddy is talking to her.''

"But you didn't."

He shrugged. "Her listening skills will improve with age, don't you think?"

"I'm certain of it. Or at least, they will until she's twelve or thirteen. And then, for at least ten years, she won't listen to a single thing you say."

"That's encouraging."

"It's called being a teenager. Luckily most of them grow out of it. So you put her down?"

"That's right. I put her in her crib." He looked enormously pleased with himself. A swatch of shiny dark hair had fallen over his forehead. Hannah kept both hands on her coffee cup. That way she couldn't reach out and smooth it back into place.

He leaned against the door frame. She realized he was looking down—at her feet. "Ms. Miller, do you have something against wearing shoes?"

She shouldn't encourage him, and she knew it, but somehow, "They cramp my style" just popped out of her mouth. She qualified, quickly, "However, I am aware that a grown-up person can't just go around barefoot all the time."

He looked at her sideways. "You are?"

"I am. So I don't. But in my own room—" She caught herself. This *was* his house. Maybe he had some objection to her going barefoot in it. If he wanted his baby's nanny to wear shoes, well fine. She'd wear shoes.

"Ms. Miller, what are you thinking?"

"Well, I have reconsidered. It's your house. And for now, I'm your baby's nanny. If you don't want to see me barefoot, I'll make a concentrated effort to keep my shoes on, even in my room.''

"Ms. Miller, I wouldn't dream of cramping your personal style. I'll trust your judgment and discretion on the subject of when or when not to wear your shoes."

She rather liked the sound of that, so she granted him a big, happy smile and sipped some more coffee.

He said, "I was just curious, that's all."

"Well, okay. So now you know."

"I'll be back at eleven. You and Becky will be ready?"

"You bet. See you then."

Cord appeared right on time. He'd changed into soft, khaki-colored trousers and a forest-green polo shirt, with a pair of crepe-soled suede bucks on his feet. Hannah thought he looked incredibly handsome in his casual clothes—but not very much like a Texan.

She probably shouldn't have, but she teased him about that.

"All you need is a cashmere sweater tossed across your shoulders—with the arms tied around your neck…"

"All I need is a cashmere sweater *and…?*"

"—And you'll look like somebody from Massachusetts. Somebody who spends his summers on Martha's Vineyard. Somebody who—"

"I get your point, Ms. Miller. For your information, I have been known to wear Tony Lamas, a Stetson and a string tie now and then."

"I'll believe it when I see it."

He gave her a long-suffering look, then suggested, "Shall we go?"

"Absolutely."

They went down the stairs at the end of the hall and out through the door at the west end of the mansion. Once outside, they stopped under an oak, to open up the stroller and get Becky situated comfortably inside, with the little shade in its proper place, open and shielding her from the bright morning sun.

"Do I get to push?" he asked, looking so unassuming and hopeful that Hannah's foolish heart melted just a little.

"Of course you do. Where shall we go?"

"How about down to Stockwell Pond? It's past the tennis courts and the stables in back."

She shot him a doubtful glance. "How many miles?"

"It's not *that* far. We can take this path." He pointed toward a walkway with trees on either side of it. "It curves around the formal gardens—or we can go through them, if you want. When we get to the pond, we'll see how Becky's doing. We can walk a little farther—there's a path along the water's edge—or come on back to the house."

"Let's go through the gardens."

"Your wish is my command."

Oh, she liked the sound of that…way too much.

She hung back for a moment as he started pushing Becky along the path, thinking that she was getting much too friendly with him, that she enjoyed his company a lot more than she'd ever expected to—or ought to be allowing herself to.

Could there be trouble in the making here?

Oh, don't be a darn fool, Hannah scoffed at herself.

She'd seen those pictures of him in the society pages. Seen the kind of woman he always had on his arm. Not a barefoot pump jockey's daughter in the bunch.

He was just a natural flirt, that was all. He did it without thinking about it. It came to him like breathing came to other men. It didn't mean a thing to him.

And as long as she kept that in mind, she could just relax and enjoy herself with him. Why shouldn't she? Having a little fun with him would only make the time they spent in each other's company more agreeable for both of them.

As she reasoned all this out with herself, the man in question and his daughter had moved several yards down the path. He glanced back. "Coming?"

She hurried to keep up.

They strolled under the pleasant shade of the trees for a while, orioles and jays warbling at them from the branches overhead. Once, Hannah looked up and spotted a gorgeous red cardinal. It flew off just as she spied it, a crimson streak against the blue Texas sky.

In the distance, she could hear the low drone of an engine. Through the trees, she picked out the source: a man in a broad-brimmed hat, cutting the grass on a riding mower. No doubt it took more than one of those machines to groom all the lawns at Stockwell Mansion.

They passed the tennis courts first. There were two of them, surrounded by a high cyclone fence. Cord pointed out the stables when they strolled by them: a long clapboard building with a green roof. Beyond the stables, behind a white fence, a pair of bay horses nibbled grass and swatted flies with their thick reddish tails.

"Do you ride, Ms. Miller?"

"Not if I can help it, Mr. Stockwell."

"An Oklahoma girl who can't ride a horse?"

"Not every Oklahoma girl's a cowgirl."

"How about tennis? Do you play?"

"Never have found the time, to tell you the truth."

"What sports *do* you enjoy?"

"Well, I like double-deck Air Force pinochle—is that a sport? And I bowl."

"You bowl."

"You bet. I bowl in the 170s. That's darn good, in case you didn't know."

"I know how to bowl, Ms. Miller."

"Well. A man of many talents. But what about pinochle?"

"I'm damn good at it, as a matter of fact."

She shot him a suspicious glance. He just did not look like the pinochle type.

She gave him a few specifics. "I'm talking about the game for four players, partners. You don't use the nines. You have a round of bidding and a then a round of play and you—"

"Ms. Miller. I know the game. My older brother, Jack, taught me. Years ago. He taught all three of us, as a matter of fact."

"All three...?"

"Me. Kate. And Rafe—Rafe is my twin?"

"I remember." In their early interviews, he had told her about Rafe, and mentioned that his twin worked as a Deputy U.S. Marshall. He hadn't said much about Jack at all, though—except that Jack was away from the mansion quite a bit.

Now, he said, "Jack was laid up at the time."

"He was sick?"

"Not exactly. He'd been injured—his left foot. In some small South American country—the name of the place escapes me at the moment. By the time he got medical attention his foot was the size of a foot*ball*. And he needed surgery. So they shipped him home. He had the surgery. And then it was another several weeks before he could walk. It was summer, the summer Rafe and I graduated high school. We were all at home. And Jack decided to teach us to play pinochle, as a way to ease his own boredom, I suppose, while he waited for his foot to heal.''

Cord paused on the path. His smile was a musing one. ''Jack has a soft spot for Kate, but he's never been particularly close to me or Rafe. He's the loner of the family, I guess you could say.''

Hannah thought she understood. ''It was a thrill for you and Rafe, I'll bet. To have your big brother with you all summer long.''

Cord shot her a look. ''A thrill? We were eighteen years old.''

''Oh, right. Big men.''

''We thought so.''

''So you played it cool, but deep in your hearts...''

''Hell. All right, we were thrilled.''

''And tell me. What was your brother doing in a small South American country in the first place?''

''The usual. Fighting somebody else's war.''

''He's a soldier?''

''He's a merc.''

''A merk?''

Cord grinned. ''A soldier for hire, as they say.''

''You're kidding.''

''No. My big brother is a mercenary, a fact that has always driven the old man right up the wall—but then again, everything about Jack has always driven my father right up the wall.''

''Jack was the rebellious type?''

''I suppose you could say that—not that he didn't have a damn good reason to be.''

''You're implying that your father was hard on your older brother?''

''No. My father was *hard* on the rest of us. He was— and is—nothing short of merciless when it comes to

Jack.'' Cord paused again, and then slanted her a glance with suspicion in it. ''Why am I telling you all this?''

''Because I'm interested. And people say I'm easy to talk to.''

''I never would have guessed it. Until very recently.''

''You saw one side of me—the side that had to make sure Becky got everything she needed.''

''And *are* you sure now?''

''I'm getting there.''

He shook his dark head. ''You don't give an inch, do you?''

''I said I'm getting there.''

They had stopped walking again, there on the path, under the shade of a sweet gum tree. The sun shone down through the leaves, creating patterns of brightness and shadow, bringing out hints of warm brown in his dark hair, glinting off the silver strands at his temples. His eyes gleamed at her.

A breeze stirred the branches overhead. Something touched her hair, near her ear. She started to lift her hand, to brush it away.

He said, ''Wait...''

She froze. His eyes...

All the words for blue went tumbling through her mind. Cerulean, indigo, sapphire, cyan.

''It's a leaf,'' he whispered. ''A leaf in your hair...''

''I'll get it.''

''No.'' He caught her hand.

His touch was light—but not his grip. She couldn't have broken his hold if she had wanted to. It was warm, his hand. Hot, even. Yes. Hot. The heat moved out. Starting from where he was touching her, radiating through her hand, out the tips of her fingers. And the other way, too.

Down her arm to her elbow, up to her shoulder and over, across her collarbone, down the other arm.

Down.

Yes, it was going all through her.

Down into the very center of her.

She sighed, though she knew she shouldn't have. She could hear Becky making baby talk, chattering away in nonsense syllables.

And the words for blue were still with her, a low chant inside her mind. Azure, aquamarine, navy, cobalt—and that exotic one, the one that started with an *L.* What was that one? Oh, yes. Lapis lazuli.

He said, "Let me…"

And all she could make herself do was nod.

Chapter Six

It was nothing, she kept trying to tell herself later.

A leaf in her hair.

A teasingly gallant gesture on the part of a man who enjoyed women more than he ought to.

Nothing. He freed the leaf, held it out for her to see, five-pointed, turning gold, the points curling inward like the wrinkled fingers of an aged hand.

"Just a leaf," he said again.

And then he dropped it to the path. She stared down at it, feeling the heat in her face, thinking that the day, too warm before, had suddenly become downright hot.

Too hot.

Becky started to fuss.

Hannah saw her opportunity to escape and went for it. "She probably needs changing. We should go back."

"We haven't even reached the gardens yet."

She looked at him then. Right into his eyes, thinking, just blue. That's all. Blue.

Forget all those other words for it. Forget I ever thought of them. "I want to go back."

For a moment that seemed to last forever and a day, he looked at her. It felt terribly intimate, the way that he stared. In her mind's eye, she saw herself. As she had been once. So young. So alone. So hungry for... connection. For someone to call her own. She had trusted unwisely. And the cost had been very high. Almost high enough to destroy her. That couldn't happen again. And it wouldn't. She knew better now.

She reached for the stroller, pushed it around in a circle, to take the crying baby back to the house. But Cord Stockwell was blocking the path.

Her heart had set up a ruckus inside her chest and she was sweating, suddenly, clammy and uncomfortable beneath her arms, under her breasts.

"You're in the way," she said.

"Don't you want to see the pond where my mother and my uncle drowned?"

She blinked, sure she hadn't heard him right. "I don't...what?"

And maybe she hadn't, because the next thing he said, quite mildly, was, "Never mind. You're right. It's time we went back."

He moved out of the path and fell in step with her as she pushed the stroller toward the edifice of brick and gleaming white masonry that loomed so large against the Texas sky.

Hannah saw two nanny candidates that afternoon. They both seemed nice enough. And they had good references.

But neither was quite right.

The older one, a Mrs. Henchly, came across as just a tiny bit cold. And the younger one, Alicia Midland, had a nervous habit of crossing one leg over the other and bouncing her foot as she talked. Hannah wondered if Becky might pick up such a habit, if she were exposed to it on a round-the-clock basis.

So she thanked both applicants and sent them on their way.

After they left, she wondered if she was being too picky. Probably. But then again, when it came to Becky, how could she go wrong by wanting the best? And this was only the first day of interviews, after all. She'd see several applicants tomorrow. No doubt the right one would be among them.

Cord stayed away for the rest of the day. That was just fine with Hannah. Those moments beneath the sweet gum tree had unnerved her. She kept telling herself she was reading way too much into the incident. But then she'd recall the way he'd looked at her, the heat in his touch— and in his eyes...

No. The more he stayed away, the better, as far as she was concerned.

She needed to find the nanny, the *right* nanny, that was all. And then she wouldn't have to worry about Mr. Cord Stockwell anymore.

Still, she did wonder about him.

Had he really said that, about his mother and his uncle drowning in the pond? Or had she only imagined it?

No. She couldn't have imagined it. No way would her mind just dream up something like that.

He had said it.

But was it true?

It probably wouldn't be that difficult to find out. A double drowning in a prominent family would surely have made the *Morning News*.

She could ask around. The Stockwells were the next thing to royalty in Grandview. Maybe one of the maids could tell her, if she just casually inquired—

Hannah stopped herself.

Just cut those thoughts off cold.

She'd been very careful when Becky came to her to adhere to a policy of strictest confidentiality. All the children in her care—and their families for that matter—deserved to have their privacy protected. Since the Stockwells had such a high public profile, Hannah had been even more careful than usual in this case. The news that Cord Stockwell had a daughter by the now-deceased Marnie Lott was bound to leak out eventually, but no one would ever be able to say that they had heard it from Hannah Miller.

No. She would not start gossiping about Cord or his family now.

However...

Maybe she had been just a little lax in her research. Maybe, for Becky's sake, she should have dug a little deeper into the background of the Stockwell family. She could pay a visit to the library, take a look at a few back issues of the *Morning News* on microfiche...

She caught herself again, and muttered aloud, "For heaven's sake, why not just *ask* the man? He's answered every other question you've asked him up till now."

Maybe she ought to be just a little bit honest with herself here. Whatever had happened to his mother and his uncle in the past had no bearing on Cord Stockwell's current ability to take care of his child. It was nothing that called for *research*.

Hannah was simply curious, that was all—about Cord Stockwell's family. And about the man himself.

She wanted to know more about him.

And that worried her. It worried her a lot.

Cord called Jerralyn that afternoon.

He made a date with her for dinner that evening—at her house. It seemed a very good idea to him, to spend a little time with Jerralyn. She could be extremely diverting.

And he needed a little diverting—from what, he wasn't even going to let himself think about.

He worked until eight on a number of different projects. And then he went upstairs to shower and change. It was after nine when he knocked on the door of Jerralyn's house in exclusive Turtle Creek.

She had set a fine table. There was filet mignon and slivered carrots with almonds. Cord had brought a couple of bottles of good Merlot. They ate by candlelight. After the meal, they sat in her living room, sipping more wine, talking.

Eventually Jerralyn set her wineglass on the coffee table and leaned close. "I've been waiting for this moment all day," she whispered. She smelled of expensive perfume and something else, something that up until now had excited him, a hot scent, and a willing one.

He set his own wineglass aside and kissed her.

The kiss went on for a long time. But it was no use. Somehow, he couldn't quite manage to lose himself in it.

Strange. Jerralyn was a gorgeous, clever, extremely sexual woman. She should have held his interest for at least a month or two. But now his mind kept wandering, kept leading him off to other places. Like the nursery, where his baby girl was probably sleeping right now, sighing, turning her little face toward the wall.

He should have stopped in there, this evening, before he came here. He'd *wanted* to stop in there. Too damn much.

There lay the problem.

The nursery held...other attractions, beyond his beautiful little girl.

Dangerous attractions.

A saucy tongue. Wide green eyes. Chestnut hair. Slim bare feet...

What the hell was going on here? He didn't get it. The social worker was not his type. Not his type at all. Too wholesome, too mouthy, too plain old down-home. And to make the situation doubly impossible, she *worked* for him.

The woman in his arms—who was *exactly* his type—pulled away. "Cord. What is it?"

He realized he couldn't stay. "I'm sorry, Jerralyn." He stood. "I shouldn't have come here."

"What the hell is going on?"

"Forgive me." He turned for the door.

"Wait."

He looked back at her and found himself thinking in a distant way that she really was stunning—in a shell-pink slip dress that barely covered the essentials, her long blond hair falling over her shoulders, her perfect face flushed, her lips soft and full.

She said, "If you leave this house now, Cord Stockwell, don't even let yourself imagine that I'll ever speak to you again."

"I'm sorry to hear that. But I certainly understand. Good night, Jerralyn."

It was almost eleven when he reached the mansion. He'd driven the Aston Martin that night. He left the car in the front driveway for one of the chauffeurs to deal with and entered the house through the main entrance, beneath the South Portico. Inside, he proceeded up the circular central stairway, then on through the big upper hall, and finally down the slightly narrower corridor with the row of doors to the nursery on one side and his sitting room on the other.

All three nursery doors were shut—the one to the nanny's room, and the playroom and Becky's bedroom door as well. Anger flared inside him when he saw all those shut doors. Shut against him. Or at least, it felt that way right then.

There was only one remedy for a shut door, he decided: to open it. He chose Becky's bedroom, grasping the brass handle, turning it, pushing the door wide.

The room was dim, but not dark. The little carousel lamp over the changing table cast a soft pool of light across the star-dusted rug.

Ms. Miller sat in the rocker. If she'd been rocking a moment ago, she wasn't now. She sat very still, regarding him through wary eyes, her hair like a soft dark cloud around her pale face. She wore her white gown and her green robe and, as usual, nothing on her feet. She held Becky in her arms. His little girl was avidly sucking at a bottle.

He stepped over the threshold and shut the door behind him. "I'd like to feed her." He approved of the tone of his own voice. None of the anger and frustration he felt could be heard in it at all. He sounded calm, confident.

Like the one in command—which he was.

Ms. Miller stood. He went to her. She passed him the baby. It was a little awkward, but they managed it without Becky ever losing her greedy grip on the nipple. During the exchange, his right hand grazed a soft left breast. The contact sent heat sizzling through him.

She must have felt it, too. He heard her quick, indrawn breath—which she released a moment later, slowly, with care.

Once he had Becky, Ms. Miller edged to the side, out of his way. He turned and took her place in the rocker.

She stood a few feet away. She looked slightly lost, as if she didn't know quite what to say.

Fine. Let her look just a little bit lost. She'd always been too sure of herself by half, anyway.

He gazed down at his daughter. That girl knew how to eat, her tiny mouth working away, an expression of near-ecstasy on her sweet little face. He smiled at her, readjusted the bottle a fraction higher, so the formula would drain more freely.

Ms. Miller chose that moment to speak. "Well, if you're all right, I'll just—"

He looked up, into those green eyes. What was it he saw in them? Apprehension? A hint of panic? Good. "Got a diaper?"

"Of course."

She took the one from her shoulder and handed it to him. He let her hold it out for a few awkward seconds before he took it from her, enjoying her discomfort more than any decent man would. He smoothed it in place on his own shoulder. "Thanks."

"No problem. Now, if you—"

He had no intention of letting her leave just yet. "Any luck this afternoon?"

"Luck?"

"You said you had interviews."

"Oh. Yes. Two."

"And?"

"They were...not quite right."

"Neither of them?"

"Yes. I mean, no. They weren't."

"Well. You'll have better luck tomorrow."

"Yes, I'm sure of that."

He looked down at Becky again.

And Ms. Miller said, "Well, I suppose I'll just—"

No, he thought. You won't. "Are you taking Becky out walking again, tomorrow?"

"I—"

"We should go earlier, I think. It'll be cooler."

"Um, *we?*"

"Say, around nine-thirty?"

"I..."

"It's settled then." He gave her a smile. Her pretty mouth stretched in response, stiffly, unwillingly. He said, "Maybe we'll make it all the way to the pond tomorrow."

She blinked. "The pond?"

"Yes. The pond." He knew damn well what she was thinking. "Go ahead. Ask."

"I..." She caught her lower lip between her teeth, worried it, then let it go. "Well, it...surprised me, what you said this morning."

"About my mother and my uncle?"

She nodded. She had her arms wrapped around herself, a defensive stance. But she was curious. She wanted to know more. For the moment, she'd forgotten all about leaving.

He hid his self-satisfied smile. "It's the truth. Or at least, it's what my father always told us. It happened almost thirty years ago—twenty-nine, to be exact. Kate was just a year old. Rafe and I were four, Jack was six."

Her eyes went darker. He saw tenderness there. "You were all so young. It must have been awful for you."

He let her expression of sympathy pass without remark. "They were out in a rowboat together. There were rumors that they were lovers, sneaking off to steal a few moments alone."

Cord watched her smooth throat move above that innocent white ruffle as she swallowed. "Your mother and your uncle...?"

"Yes. Lovers. Or at least, that's how the story goes. Uncle Brandon was my father's twin, did you know?"

"No. I...I've never heard any of this before."

"Twins seem to run in the family."

"That's right. Like you and your brother, Rafe."

He nodded. "The boat must have capsized."

"Must have?"

Becky had drained the bottle. She pulled off the nipple and her little face screwed up, an expression Cord already recognized as one of discomfort—or possibly displeasure.

"Here," said Ms. Miller, extending her hand.

He gave her the bottle, and then lifted Becky to his shoulder. She snuggled up, her little body relaxing now that he'd put her in a better position. Within seconds, she burped.

He gently rubbed her back—and dished out a little more family dirt for Ms. Miller to ponder. "The bodies were never found."

Ms. Miller wrapped her arms around herself again, still holding Becky's empty bottle in one hand. "Never found? In a pond? A pond can't be that big."

"This pond is. You'll see tomorrow. It's a couple of miles across at its broadest point. And over thirty feet deep in some places."

"But wouldn't they have dredged...for the bodies?"

"Ms. Miller. I told you. I was four years old. I don't remember the details that clearly."

"And I'd imagine you don't really *want* to remember."

"What is that supposed to mean?"

"Just that most of us want to put painful events behind us. We try not to dwell on them. We get on with our lives."

"Are you speaking from experience?"

Her gaze shifted briefly away—but she didn't answer his question, just continued on with her own line of reasoning. "I'm only saying that it's a little...farfetched, that's all. The bodies should have turned up eventually. Maybe something else happened."

He gave her a cold smile. "Are you suggesting foul play?"

"I'm not suggesting anything. Just telling you what I think."

"You do that a lot. Say just what you think."

Her chin went up. "You don't like it?"

"Ms. Miller." He let out a long breath. "I like it just fine."

That took the wind out of her sails. "Well," she said. "All right."

Becky chose that moment to squirm and let out a low groan. A moment later, when the odor hit him, he realized what had just happened.

"Ugh," he said.

Ms. Miller chuckled. Why was it she always got such pleasure out of seeing him at a loss?

"The time has come at last," she announced.

He stood from the rocker and held out the baby. "You can do it."

She pointed at the changing bureau. "No, *you* can do it. I'll be here, though. For backup. If you really need it."

Since the damn woman wouldn't take her, he was

forced to carry Becky over to the bureau and lay her down.

"You show no mercy, Ms. Miller."

"Stop complaining. I'll help if you really need it."

And she did. That is, she supervised, though she made him do everything himself. It was not the most fun he'd ever had. But he got through it.

He carried Becky back to the rocker when it was done, and put her against his shoulder again. She cuddled up and sighed.

Ms. Miller said softly, "She'll be asleep in five minutes."

He rocked a little, holding his daughter close, enjoying the silence. It seemed a reasonably comfortable silence now. And Ms. Miller appeared to have forgotten all about how much she wanted to get away from him.

"Your father..." Ms. Miller began, after two or three minutes of quiet.

"My father what?"

"He sounds like a very troubled man."

"Troubled." Cord thought about that word, then let out a low, humorless laugh. "If he knew someone had called him that, he'd be insulted."

"Why?"

"Men like my father are not 'troubled.' Men like my father are tough. You don't go against my father unless you're ready to fight till you plain can't fight anymore. He's tough in a business negotiation. And he's tough on his family, as I think I've mentioned more than once—or at least, he *was* tough. Now, with the cancer, he's...not the same. And the past keeps coming back to haunt him. He babbles about it, crazy stuff that doesn't make a lot of sense."

"He talks about the boating accident?"

"Yeah. Among other things." He slanted her a measuring look, wondering how much she could take. How comfortable with him she really was, right then.

The dim room, the warmth of the small body against his chest, the companionable silence they had recently shared…they all conspired to make him say more than he would ordinarily have revealed.

"They say I'm like him."

"Like your father?"

"That's right."

"Who is 'they'?"

"People who know us both."

"How are you like him?"

"Well, first in the obvious way. Rafe and I look just like him…or at least, the way he used to look."

"And?"

"And I'm a damn good businessman myself. And then there are…"

She was leaning against the changing table. She stood a little straighter, curiosity gleaming in those eyes of hers. "There are what?"

"All the women."

She pulled back—just marginally. "The women."

"That's right. He cheated on my mother. Repeatedly. With a number of different women. I've heard that from more than one source—including my father himself. And after my mother died, there was an endless string of girl-friends. None of them lasted very long. He didn't have it in him to be true to any one woman. He used to make the papers, too, in his day. I remember the pictures of him, at this or that gala event—always with a different woman on his arm. Sound familiar?"

Had he wanted to get under her skin? Scare her off?

Or maybe just remind her of exactly the kind of man he was?

He wasn't sure.

But her reaction surprised him. She asked softly, with a tender sort of irony, "What are you tryin' to say here, that womanizing is a genetic disorder?"

He stared at her mouth, thinking how much he wanted to kiss it. She'd been living in his house for less than forty-eight hours. And already he was wondering how he ever could have imagined he didn't want her in his bed.

"I think I'm saying that a man learns what he lives."

"And can't a man learn *from* the mistakes his father has made?"

"That would be the ideal, I suppose. But this is the real world."

"You are a cynic."

"A realist."

"A man *can* change, Cor—" she caught herself "—Mr. Stockwell."

"We've just done a loaded diaper together. I think it's time we got on a first-name basis with each other."

She had her arms wrapped around herself again. "Maybe that's not such a good idea."

He gazed back at her steadily. "Nothing's going to happen between us, Hannah."

She gave him that wary-bird look of hers, from the side. "You're right about that."

"I...enjoy talking to you. In spite of how strongly you disapprove of me, I think you're learning to like me a little, too."

"You certainly aren't lackin' when it comes to self-confidence."

"Be straight. Do you...like me a little?"

She took several seconds to answer. "All right. Yes. But that is as far as it's going to go."

"I think we already agreed on that point." He glanced toward the baby on his shoulder. "She's asleep..."

"Yes." Her voice had gone whisper-soft again. "Out like a light."

Carefully he rose from the rocker. He carried his daughter to her crib and gently laid her down.

"Hannah?"

She had tiptoed as far as the doorway to the playroom. She stopped, looked back at him, waiting.

"If your parents aren't in Oologah, where are they?"

Her eyes had shadows in them again. "My parents are in heaven."

"They're dead."

She looked down at those pretty, pale feet, then right back up at him again. "Since I was nine. After that, until I was old enough to take care of myself, I lived in foster homes."

"And now you work for Child Protective Services because you want to help kids in need—as you once were."

"Pretty classic, huh?"

"Understandable. Your job requires at least a four-year degree, doesn't it?"

"That's right. And I've got one. From OSU. It wasn't easy. I had to work my way through, and I've only paid off the last of my student loans a few months ago."

"Good for you."

She started to turn again.

He couldn't quite let her go. "Just tell me..."

"What?"

"Your parents. How did they die?"

Her eyes sparked. With anger. Or maybe hurt. "What

is this? You want us to be even? Your mother and uncle—for my mom and dad?"

"No. I'd like to know, that's all."

She looked at him for a long time. And then she said, "My dad died in an explosion at the station. A careless customer and a lighted cigarette. He was standing right by the pump. My mother went six months later. They said it was pneumonia. But I knew it was a broken heart. There never were two people so in love as my mama and daddy."

"You miss them."

"Always. They were—"

Right then, a phone began to ring in the sitting room across the hall.

"It's in your rooms," Hannah said.

He felt bone-weary all of a sudden. "Probably my father." At this time of night, who else would it be? Except Jerralyn, possibly, calling to tell him what a bastard he was.

"You'd better answer it," Hannah said.

He nodded and left her, dreading what he'd have to deal with when he picked up the phone—and already looking forward to the morning.

He'd stop in at the nursery again good and early, before he went downstairs. Early enough to feed Becky her bottle. He'd probably end up having to deal with another smelly diaper. But he could handle it. He'd done it once and lived to tell about it.

And Hannah would be there, to help, if he needed her.

Chapter Seven

It was one of Caine's nurses calling.

Cord said he'd be right there.

He spent an hour in the oppressive splendor of his father's rooms, as Caine alternately dozed and ranted. It was more of the same, the facts of the past all mixed up with an old man's guilt and sick confusion. He railed about the baby, the one he said had been born almost thirty years ago, about his twin brother and his long-dead wife, about how Madelyn had betrayed him—or maybe hadn't betrayed him. How she'd run off with Brandon. Much of what he said was gibberish, impossible to follow.

He got going eventually on some long-ago land deal. Something that apparently had happened at the turn of the last century, during the time when the first Caine Stockwell, Cord's great-grandfather, had been in charge.

Caine pulled on Cord's arm and confided in a whining, raspy whisper, "Over sixty years had gone by. What was

done was done. Why the hell couldn't Brandon just leave
it alone?'' Something struck him as funny. He laughed,
an ugly rheumy laugh. ''Besides, Miles Johnson must
have been a damn fool, easy to fleece as a lost baby
lamb.''

Miles Johnson. Cord knew the name. He'd been Madelyn's grandfather, and the first Caine's contemporary.

''All right,'' Caine muttered, closing his eyes, beginning to toss his head on the pillow. ''He was a hard man,
my grandfather Caine. He took what he wanted. He took
the land. Miles Johnson should have watched his
back…Miles Johnson was born to lose what he had.'' The
red-rimmed eyes were open again—and focused on Cord.
Cord thought he saw madness in their depths. ''You tell
me. How many brats did he father? Seven? Eight? And
how many are left now of that line? Hell. Weak blood.''
Caine coughed, several times, lifting his head off the pillow, then finally dropping back with a weary, rattling sigh.

He waved one skeletal hand. ''Deserved what they got,
those Johnsons, hell if they didn't. You hold what's yours
or you lose it, it's a simple fact of life.'' Caine muttered
a few low words Cord couldn't make out, then grabbed
Cord's arm again and demanded, ''Didn't we employ 'em,
those Johnsons? We gave 'em work. Madelyn's mother,
Emily, didn't she run the house for us? And then later, it
was Madelyn herself. Little housekeeper. Sneakin' off to
meet with Brandon…always Brandon. I made her my
wife. But she never stopped loving *him*. The witch. The
sweet-faced, wide-eyed witch…''

The bony fingers dug into Cord's flesh. ''Brandon
thought we should make restitution. Restitution. Hah.
Hah, hah, hah…'' He coughed, and the cough took over,
the spasms racking his wasted frame.

''Easy,'' Cord said. ''Easy now. Breathe.''

The coughing fit passed. Caine flopped back to the pillows. "God. Hate this."

Cord asked, carefully, "So you're saying that Great-Grandfather Caine cheated Miles Johnson out of—"

"What?" Caine shot to a sitting position again. "Cheated? I don't like the sound of that word. No one was cheated. I don't know what the hell you're talking about, son."

"Dad. You said—"

"Tired now." Caine fell back again. "Hurting. Help me. The pain..." The old man's eyes drooped shut. He groaned, rolled his head back and forth. "I need my medicine. I need it now."

Cord rang for the nurses. They came within seconds. This time, Caine was calm enough to receive his dosage orally. Cord helped him, holding his head, placing the pills on his tongue, tipping the glass to his slack, pale lips.

"Stay with me. Need you..." Caine whispered as Cord gently lowered his head to the pillow once more. "My boy. Just like me. You'll carry on. My blood. Stockwell blood. You'll see that we always keep what's ours."

Hannah came to Becky's room at seven the next morning to find Cord standing over the crib.

Cord...but somehow *not* Cord.

The clothes were all wrong, for starters. Western-cut slacks, and a tan sport coat, cowboy boots and a pearl-gray hat—a Stetson from the look of it.

He'd taken the hat off and held it in his left hand, against his lean thigh.

He stared down at Becky, a slightly bewildered expression on his face. Becky, awake and quite contented at that moment, gurgled and cooed and waved her little hands at him.

Hannah hesitated at the threshold and Cord glanced up.

One look in those eyes, which were exactly the right shade of blue—just not Cord's eyes—and she knew.

"You must be Rafe."

That mouth that wasn't quite Cord's mouth curved in a hint of a smile. "And you're the new nanny."

"For a few days, anyway." She padded toward him across the starry rug, her hand outstretched. His grip was iron-firm, like Cord's. And also, like Cord's, strangely gentle. The only thing missing was the irritating shiver of awareness Cord's touch always inspired in her. "I'm Hannah Miller."

He frowned. "Hannah? Wait a minute. Aren't you—?"

"—That annoying social worker I told you about."

It was Cord, standing in the doorway to the hall. Hannah's heart stuttered in her chest.

Rafe turned toward his twin. "'Mornin'."

Cord replied with a nod. "Little brother."

Rafe sent a put-upon glance Hannah's way. "He's eight minutes older. You'd think it was years."

Cord, resplendent in linen slacks and a dress shirt of lustrous, cream-colored silk, entered the baby's room. "You just get home?"

"A few minutes ago. I was going to go check on the old man first. But then I remembered that the baby was supposed to be moved in by now, so I came straight up here, to see if I could get a look."

Cord moved closer to Hannah—too close, actually. "I think the new uncle wants to hold his niece."

Oh, what was the matter with her? Just the touch of that blue gaze seemed to send little flares of excitement shooting along the surface of her skin. It was bothersome in the extreme. He moved even closer. Now she could smell that wonderful aftershave he wore.

He glanced down at her bare feet. "No cramping of your personal style this morning, I see."

That irked her a little. "I told you, if it bothers you—"

"Did I say I was bothered?"

"Bothered about what?" Rafe asked.

Hannah felt her face flame. For a second there, with Cord so close, she'd almost forgotten his brother was in the room.

"Nothing." Cord's shrug was easy, completely unconcerned. "Just a little joke between Hannah and me."

Rafe looked from Cord to Hannah and then back to Cord. "I see."

What, exactly, did Rafe Stockwell see? Hannah didn't think she wanted to know. She changed the subject by moving toward the crib.

Rafe realized what she meant to do. He started backing away. "Uh...now, let's not get too hasty, here. That baby's a beauty all right, but I don't know if I—"

"Give me that hat." Cord pulled the Stetson from his brother's hand. "And your weapon, too."

Weapon? Hannah eyed Rafe with new wariness. Then she remembered. Rafe was a Deputy U.S. Marshall. A man with that kind of job would carry a gun as a matter of course.

Rafe grunted. "I've got sense enough not to bring a loaded weapon into a baby's room." He smoothed back the left front panel of his jacket, revealing an empty holster strapped to his side. "I'm clean—and if you're going to put that baby in my arms, you'd better do it now."

Cord let out a low laugh. "Before you turn and run?"

"I'm going nowhere." Rafe held out both hands, palms down. "See. Not a quiver. Nerves of steel."

Maybe his hands weren't shaking, but the look in his eyes told Hannah the man could use a little reassurance. "Holding a baby is nothing to be scared of. And it's good to practice a little, anyway."

Rafe didn't get it. "Practice for what?"

"Well, for the day when you have one of your own."

Rafe shook his head. "Too dangerous. If you don't mind, I think I'll just stick to apprehending federal fugitives and transporting serial killers across state lines."

She held out the baby. "Come on. Here you go."

Carefully, as if Becky's small body were made of something so fragile, a sudden move might break her in two, Rafe took his niece in his big arms. He looked down at her and she smiled up at him.

"Well," he said, shaking his head. "What do you know? It really is true. My brother's a daddy." He glanced over and caught Cord's eye. The two grinned their identical grins at each other.

And right then, Becky started to fuss.

Rafe looked crushed. "What did I *do?*"

Hannah waved a hand. "Nothing. She's just hungry. If her crying bothers you, give her to Cord. I'll get her some breakfast." She left them, heading for the playroom and the small kitchen area there.

When she returned with the warmed bottle of formula, Rafe had vanished and Cord was pacing the floor, his daughter wailing on his shoulder. Hannah noted with approval that he'd remembered the diaper this time. He sent her a lowering glance. "Hurry up. I think she's damaged my eardrums."

"The price of fatherhood."

"Just give me that bottle." He sat in the rocker. Hannah handed the bottle over. He plugged Becky's yowling mouth with it.

The resulting silence was absolutely lovely. The two adults enjoyed several blissful seconds without either of them uttering a word.

"That's the thing about babies," Hannah observed at last. "They teach you to appreciate the simple things— like a little peace and quiet. Where did your brother go?"

Cord pointed at the door. "That way. Fast."

"He'll be back."

"I don't know. He looked pretty nervous about all this."

"So were you. At first."

They shared a long glance. A way too friendly one, Hannah realized after it went on for a while.

She shook herself. "I'll just go ring for my breakfast."

Cord said nothing. But she felt his eyes on her as she went out the door.

He came for them at nine-thirty, just as he'd said he would.

They went down the stairs and out the west entrance, pausing as they had the day before, in the shade of an oak, to settle Becky into the stroller.

There was a nice breeze—not the usual rough, hot Texas wind—and it was still reasonably cool. They strolled down the path, under the dappling shadows of the trees, past the tennis courts and the stables. Sprinklers were going, over some sections of the lawn. The breeze carried the wetness. It felt cool and welcome misting against Hannah's cheeks.

In the garden, there were wildflowers—Indian blanket and spider lilies, strawberry cactus and tiny wild violets— as well as roses, beds of zinnias and, in the shady spots,

Hosta lilies and blankets of red, white and pink impatiens, too.

They wandered the garden path for fifteen or twenty minutes, emerging at last through a rose-covered arch onto an open stretch of lawn. The path took them down a gentle slope to the edge of Stockwell Pond.

Cord had said it was big, for a pond. He hadn't exaggerated. The trees—willows and oaks, mostly—grew close to the bank around much of the perimeter, no doubt obscuring any number of inlets and secluded spots. The water was a very deep blue, especially out toward the center. The path from the garden led down to a wooden dock with a small green-roofed boathouse perched near the end. A few yards from the dock, the path split to the left and right. The shoreline trail meandered along the water's edge, eventually vanishing into the greenery in both directions.

Cord was pushing the stroller. He headed for a stone bench, which waited invitingly under a big, old willow tree. Hannah glanced at the baby. The walk had put her to sleep.

"She's out," Cord said softly. "She won't mind if we sit for a few minutes."

Hannah hesitated. They should probably get back.

Cord didn't say anything more. He only waited for her to make up her mind.

She took a seat on the bench.

He sat beside her. They'd fallen into an easy silence with each other as they strolled through the garden. Now it just seemed natural to sit quietly, enjoying the rare mild breeze and the sparkle of sun rays that danced on the water as the breeze skimmed the surface. It seemed impossible that anyone could ever have drowned here, in such a peaceful, beautiful place.

"What was your mother like?" The question seemed to ask itself, though it was Hannah's mouth that had formed it.

She half expected him not to answer, to remain silent beside her, staring off, as she was, over the water. It would have been easy for both of them to pretend that she hadn't spoken at all.

But then he said, "Blue eyes, like the rest of us. Dark hair…"

"Did she resemble Kate?"

"Yes. But she had…a different style. She wore soft, flowing dresses. And big straw hats in the sun. She was gentle. And good to us. And she liked to paint. I have memories…images, really. Of her. Out here, by the pond. Sitting at what I didn't know at the time was an easel. I see her arm outstretched to the canvas, the loose sleeve of her dress falling away from her elbow, a brush in her hand…" His voice trailed off.

She glanced at him, then followed the direction of his gaze, back out over the pond where a mallard circled— and then descended in a beating of wings, webbed feet outstretched. It broke the surface of the water, took a moment to preen and then settled in, smoothly tucking its wings.

Cord added, "I think she was pretty good, as an artist, though how would I know that? It's just a feeling I have…"

Out on the pond, a second mallard joined the first. Hannah waited until both birds drifted smoothly on the water before she said, "You miss her."

"Doubtful." His voice, warm as the morning breeze a moment before, had a chill in it now. "I told you, Rafe and I were very young when she left."

"Left?"

"Excuse me. Drowned."

"So you *do* have some doubt that there was a drowning?"

"Lately I have doubts about a lot of things."

"Because of your father, because of the things he keeps telling you?"

"That's right."

"You could…check into what really happened. You could look up old newspaper accounts, ask someone else who was there at the time."

He looked mildly amused. "In my copious free time?"

"Hire someone—a professional—to do it for you."

He didn't answer for a moment. Then he muttered, "Maybe you're right. I'll think about it."

"Have you talked with Kate and Rafe about these things your father says?"

"Yeah."

"And?"

"Hannah, it's just…babbling. I can't make much sense out of it. And neither can they. Plus, they're getting it secondhand. He only talks to me."

"Because you're his favorite."

"I guess you could call it that."

She stared at him. It was no hardship. He had that Roman-coin profile and his hair was so thick and shiny and silky-looking. Her poor fingers just itched to run themselves through it.

She tucked those fingers under her thighs to make sure they behaved and asked, "What about your uncle Brandon?"

"What about him?"

"What was *he* like?"

"I don't remember."

"Come on. You do. At least a little."

He still did not look at her. He kept staring off, over the pond. "Vague impressions. That's all."

"Tell me."

"Why?" He turned then, met her glance. She saw that there were black flecks in his eyes. Tiny pinpoints of greater darkness embedded in the deep, deep blue.

They did it again, stared at each other way too long, too intimately. And it happened once more, as it had in the nursery. Little prickles of awareness did a naughty dance along the surface of her skin.

She knew she ought to look away, get her gaze safely focused on those ducks out there, floating so serenely on the gleaming waters of the pond.

But she didn't seem to be doing what she ought to at the moment.

Cord said, "I think my uncle Brandon was…different than my father. Not as tough. Kinder. Whatever the word is. My father always scared me, when I was little. But not Uncle Brandon. I have one image. Of him kneeling beside me, talking to me, looking right at me. I don't have a clue what he was saying to me. I don't think I understood the words at the time. I remember his eyes…Stockwell blue, but not hard, not like my father's eyes."

He looked away, the movement abrupt. "It was a long time ago."

Hannah almost reached out and laid her hand over his. She caught herself just in time.

He turned to her again. "Last night you started to tell me about *your* mother. And your father. But the phone rang."

Most of her memories of her parents were good ones, memories she would gladly share.

She asked, "What do you want to know?"

"How did they meet?"

She looked out at the pond again, imagining what she had never seen. A river of bright lights, neon in the desert...

"They met in Las Vegas. At a Wayne Newton show. My mama was raised in Northern California. She was in Vegas just for a weekend, with another girl, a pal from the office where she worked. My dad was on vacation. An Oklahoma boy with four days all to himself. He'd picked Las Vegas because he'd always wanted to see the place. And also to see Wayne Newton live."

"Big Wayne Newton fans, those two. That's what you're telling me."

"I sure am. It was a sold-out dinner show, and my mother had tickets. But my dad didn't. He was wandering around out front, hoping to find someone with an extra ticket to sell."

"And your mom—?"

"You guessed it. She had one. Her girlfriend had come down with the stomach flu."

"So your mom sold your dad her extra ticket."

"That's right."

"And the rest is history."

"It was love. From the moment she spoke to him, from the moment he answered back. They spent the evening together and they got married the next day, right there in Las Vegas. And when my dad went home to Oologah, my mama went with him. I was born nine months to the day from their wedding night."

"What were their names—your mother and father?"

"Hannah and Luke."

"You were named after your mother, then?"

"That's right. After my mother and the man who brought them together. Hannah Waynette, that's me."

"Hannah Waynette." He repeated the name slowly, as

if he were turning it over, examining it in his mind. Then he nodded. "It suits you."

"Thank you."

Out on the pond, two more ducks had joined the first pair. Somewhere not far away, a jay squawked. And Hannah could hear other birds, twittering away in the trees nearby. The breeze ruffled the drooping willow branches, making the leaves quiver sweetly.

She thought, *I could sit here forever.*

And right after that, *We have been sitting here way too long.*

She said, "We should get back."

He gave her another too-intimate look. Her pulse accelerated. Her skin grew warm.

And then he shrugged. "You're probably right." He rose.

So did she. He took the stroller. They left the shade of the willow and walked, side by side, up the slope of lawn to the path. At the mansion, he helped her to get the stroller upstairs, then left to return to his offices below.

Once he was gone, Hannah put Becky, still sleeping, into her crib. Then she went to her room, kicked off her shoes and lay down on the bed. She stared up at the ceiling, half dreaming even though she was fully awake, seeing blue eyes with tiny, shining spots of blackness in them, gleaming down at her.

Chapter Eight

Hannah saw five nanny candidates that day.

And six the next day, which was Thursday. By then, three days had passed since she'd agreed to a brief stay at Stockwell Mansion.

Three days, really, wasn't all that long.

On Friday, she saw five more prospective nannies.

As on the days before, not one of them was quite what she sought. Either their references weren't good enough, or something they said or did turned Hannah off.

Becky deserved the very best. Hannah fully intended to see that she got it.

She decided that it didn't matter if it took a little longer than she had anticipated. She'd used up her vacation time, as of Friday, but so what? Cord had insisted on paying her, so it wasn't going to cost her anything to stay a little longer.

She called the office and said she'd need a week of

unpaid leave. Her supervisor didn't argue. Hannah's was a difficult, stress-filled, time-consuming job, the kind of job a person almost had to have a calling for. Hannah had a calling. And her boss at CPS knew it and didn't want to lose her. Her boss told her to enjoy her week of leave and to please report in on the morning of Monday, the twenty-fifth. She promised that she would. She felt certain that by then she would accomplish her goal.

Cord came to the nursery regularly, three or four times a day, every day. So far, he was proving himself a much more interested and involved parent than Hannah had ever imagined he might be. Hannah actually found herself growing accustomed to the little thrill that pulsed through her at the sound of his voice—not to mention at the sight of him, so big and handsome and immaculately dressed, standing in the doorway to the hall.

Sometimes, when he looked at her, she knew she was in trouble. She was far too attracted to him for her own good—and she, of all people, should know better than to succumb to the dangerously seductive charms of a man like Cord Stockwell.

But then she'd remind herself that she *hadn't* succumbed. That she never *would* succumb. That he wasn't even trying to *get* her to succumb.

They had an agreement on that issue. He had said it himself. *Nothing's going to happen between us, Hannah.*

Well, nothing *had* happened.

And nothing *would*.

Yes, sometimes he looked at her too long. And maybe she went ahead and looked right back.

But he never touched her in any way that could be considered the least inappropriate. He stayed true to his word.

Their days just naturally seemed to fall into a pleasing pattern.

He came to see his daughter first thing in the morning. Then later, around nine-thirty, they shared a stroll on the grounds. Wednesday, he dropped in again at noon and Thursday, he came a little later. Each night, he appeared around eleven, to feed Becky her final meal of the day.

Whenever he stopped in the nursery, he and Hannah inevitably seemed to end up sharing at least a few minutes of conversation. It just seemed natural that the two of them would get to talking. Strangely, after so much animosity between them at first, they talked easily now, almost like longtime companions. He told her more about his family, about what it was like growing up a Stockwell. And she chatted about her job and how much she loved it. Sometimes they argued politics—or football. The Oklahoma/Texas rivalry was an old one. They each remained loyal to their native states.

Friday afternoon, he stopped in to see Becky at a little after five. She was still sleeping.

He hung around, waiting for her to wake.

They wandered into the playroom. Hannah plunked herself down on one of the fluffy throw rugs, the one that was shaped like a big yellow sun, and gathered her legs to the side. Cord remained standing. He leaned against the blue-tiled counter in the galley area.

He asked about her childhood in Oologah. Hannah told him about the happy years, before her dad died, about the little house they lived in, a classic prairie cottage: three bedrooms, and no hallways—living room, dining room and kitchen in a row, with a bedroom branching off of each.

She remembered it so clearly, that wonderful little house. ''The bathroom was papered in yellow roses, with beaded pine wainscoting and a claw-foot tub. You had to go through one of the back bedrooms to get to it. There were lace curtains at every window in that house, and the sun shining through them made the most beautiful patterns on the old hardwood floors.

"We had a dog," she told him. "A sweet little sheltie mix. She kind of looked like a miniature collie, long nose, fox-colored fur—with white around the neck and down her belly. We called her Annie. When my mama died, a neighbor took her. I cried when I said goodbye. I can still remember the smell of her fur that last time I hugged her—you know that doggy smell, like dirt and sunshine? I remember wiping my tears on the ruff of white fur at her neck. And her swiping her long wet tongue all over my face." The memory felt almost real, as Hannah told it. She sighed and shook her head. "Sorry."

"What for?"

"I was telling you my *happy* memories. Somewhere in the middle, that one turned sad."

"Memories have a tendency to do that sometimes."

She made a low noise of agreement and asked, "What about you?"

"What *about* me?"

"Is there a dog in your past?"

He admitted there was. "A spotted pedigreed cocker, with long floppy ears and hair that was always in need of a good brushing."

"They say purebred dogs are usually high-strung."

"Not this one. He was good-natured, but I think most of the brains had been bred right out of him. His real name was Champion, but we all called him Slider. He'd run on the marble floor in the front hall and then he'd stop—and he'd slide right into the wall."

There was more—she could tell by the look on his face. "What? Tell me?"

"*We* did it, too."

"What?"

"Sliding. In the front hall—when my father wasn't around to beat the tar out of us for it, I mean. We'd get towels, from the downstairs bathrooms. Big, thick Turkish ones. And we'd lay them out in the middle of the floor. Then we'd get back and take off at a run. If you hit the towel just right, got your butt on it good and solid, you could slide a good twenty feet."

"Until you ran into the wall."

"That *was* the objective."

There was silence. They enjoyed it, together, each halfway listening for the sound of a baby waking in the other room.

Eventually she asked, "What happened to Slider?"

He shrugged. "Slider got old. I think Rafe and I were seventeen or eighteen when we had to put him down."

"'Rafe and I,'" she echoed. "You do that a lot. You don't just say how old *you* were. It's always the two of you. Is that a twin thing?"

He chuckled. "A twin *thang?*"

"There is an *a* in 'thing,' Cord Stockwell. Just like there's an *r* in 'wash'—and is it, a twin thing?"

"I suppose so. Hell. I guess we're not as spooky as some identicals. But we're spooky enough. We've been known to finish each other's sentences now and again. And you're right. When I think of my childhood, it tends to be 'Rafe and I.' He was always there, and he was always the exact same age that I was."

"Minus eight minutes."

"That's right. I'm the big brother. And I never let him

forget it. So where did you go, after your mother died, after you said goodbye to Annie?''

She told him about the group home, where kids waited to be adopted—or more likely, to get assigned to foster care. And she described her first foster home. She'd shared a bedroom there with an older girl named CindaLou. ''Poor CindaLou. She cried all the time. Looking back, it seems like she was crying every night, all night, for the entire eighteen months we stayed together in that house.''

''But *you* didn't cry. Did you, Hannah?'' There was a challenge in the words—and, she thought, a tenderness in his eyes.

She tried to ignore the tenderness and simply answer the challenge honestly. ''No, not by then. Not if I could help it. If I'd let myself, I might have started and never stopped. I learned soon enough that it was better not to even get started.''

''What about boyfriends?''

She made a show of rolling her eyes. ''Come on. I was only nine.''

''I mean later, when you were in your teens.''

For a flashing moment, in her mind's eye, she saw a certain face—young, handsome, angular, with tender blue eyes. That face stared at her with frank longing.

It was the face of betrayal.

She blinked—to banish the image and bring herself back to the here and now.

Cord was watching—way too closely. ''Sensitive subject?''

''What?''

''Boyfriends?''

''No,'' she lied, keeping her voice offhand and her expression composed. ''I didn't go out much. Never have.

For a lot of years, it took all my energy just to survive. And then I had to put my focus on getting through college. And now, well, I still don't have a lot of time for…'' She sought the right word.

He suggested, "Romance?"

That pleased her—that he hadn't said "men," or "relationships." That he'd chosen a word with adventure in it.

And excitement. And danger.

Romance.

A beautiful word.

One she should absolutely not allow herself to dwell on.

She said, "The work I do is very demanding. Any night of the week, I might get a call, just out of the blue. I have to drop everything, if a child is in danger."

"Is that what happened with Becky?"

She hastened to reassure him. "Becky wasn't in any immediate danger. A neighbor of her mother's was looking after her."

"I wasn't talking about Becky."

She frowned. "But you said—"

"I was talking about you. You mentioned dropping everything. And you did, didn't you—with Becky in particular?"

She didn't know where he was leading her. Wherever it was, she didn't think she wanted to go. She hedged, "Well, more or less. Yes."

"Why?"

"I told you. It's my job."

"But you went farther with Becky. You decided to foster her. I'm asking why. What was it about her that made her different from all the other children?"

"She needed me."

"Hannah." His tone reproached her. "They all need you. But you don't decide to foster every child assigned to you."

"No, I don't. But I—"

"You what? You rushed to her side, took one look at her and…fell in love?"

It was way too close to the truth.

And Cord knew it. "You did, didn't you? I've been curious about that. What was there about Becky that got that kind of response out of you? What would make you put all those other needy children on hold, just to take care of one?"

"I didn't put them on hold. There are other CPS workers in Grandview County, you know."

"Hannah, you took a *vacation,* to be Becky's foster mother."

"What's this? An accusation?"

"You're defensive about this. Why?"

He was right. She *was* defensive. And she had no intention of ever telling him why.

She said in a tone flat with finality, "Becky's a beautiful baby. I wanted to be able to make certain that everything worked out for her. I had some vacation time coming and I—"

He waved a hand. "You said that before. And I'm not buying. There's more going on here, there's something about my little girl that made her special to you. I just want to know what."

"There's nothing. She's a beautiful child and I—"

"Why won't you tell me?"

"Cord, I—"

"You're evading. Why?" He looked so…earnest.

Cord Stockwell. Earnest. As if he really cared. As if it really did matter to him, her secret. Her loss…

For one terrifying and heady moment, she wanted to tell him. To blurt out her whole sad little story. Her heart was beating way too hard. She could feel it, pounding in her chest, throbbing in the pulse point at her throat.

She swallowed—and pulled herself back from the brink of a confession that would do neither of them the least bit of good. "Cord. Let it be. What does it matter *why* I felt drawn to Becky? The fact is, I did. And I took time off to care for her."

There was silence again, but not a companionable one this time. This time, the silence had teeth.

And as if she could sense the tension in the air, the baby in the other room suddenly began to cry.

Cord left off leaning on the counter and moved toward the sound. Hannah stayed where she was for several minutes, staring down at the fluffy yellow rug as the cries from the other room progressed from little fussy whimpers to a full-blown wail. Finally, with a sigh, Hannah pushed herself upright and went to warm a bottle.

Chapter Nine

Cord was waiting in the doorway, Becky on his shoulder, looking aggravated, when Hannah finally got the bottle ready.

"It's about time," he muttered, laying Becky into the cradle of his left arm and grabbing the bottle out of Hannah's hand. Becky latched on to the nipple and the crying stopped.

Hannah was looking at the baby, smiling a little at the lusty way she went at her meal. Then she made the mistake of glancing up.

Cord's eyes were waiting.

She probably should have known that they would be.

He said, "Whatever you tell me, it won't go beyond these rooms."

"I know." And she did know. Over the past few days, she'd come to believe that he was a man who would keep a confidence. But what she believed and what she would act on—those had to remain two separate things.

"You're still not going to tell me," he said. "Are you?"

She shook her head.

He didn't say anything more for a number of long, way-too-enjoyable seconds. He just looked at her. And she looked back at him—the two of them, standing there in the doorway to the baby's room, staring at each other like a couple of moonstruck fools. Which was the way that they stared at each other altogether too often recently.

Disaster, Hannah thought. *I think I'm headed for disaster here. Cord had it right. I fell in love with Becky at first sight. And now…oh sweet Lord, I think I'm falling in love with Becky's daddy.*

The love for Becky, Hannah could forgive herself. But to fall for a man like Cord Stockwell…

What was that old saying? *Fool me once, shame on you. Fool me twice, shame on* me.

Yes. The shame would be all hers if she let herself get fooled again.

And even if her own past experience had failed to teach her anything, what about the words Cord himself had said to her, just four days ago?

I like them tall and I like them gorgeous—but I never like them for long.

Hannah knew she didn't fit the profile. She wasn't all that tall. And she certainly wasn't especially gorgeous. However, she had no doubt at all that whatever happened between her and Cord Stockwell wouldn't last very long.

Not that anything *would* happen between them.

"I'll get it out of you yet," he whispered. And then he smiled.

Lord. That smile could melt a girl down to a puddle of

heat and longing at twenty yards. And Hannah was standing much closer than that.

"What's going on in here?" It was Kate's voice.

Hannah jumped as if she'd been caught with her hand in the candy jar—which, in a way, she supposed she had.

Cord laughed, the sound easy, self-assured. But then, his sister had probably caught him sharing moonstruck glances with any number of women before this. He'd probably reached the point where getting caught didn't bother him at all.

Hannah turned. Kate was standing just inside the playroom, in front of the open door to the hall. Her smile gave nothing away. But the gleam in her eyes said she'd just witnessed clear signs of a budding romance.

Romance.

There was that word again. It was a word, Hannah promised herself, that she was not going to use anymore, not even in her mind.

"We're feeding Becky," Cord said. "Better get over here if you want a chance to hold her while she eats."

Kate's eyes lit up. "Oh, I do."

Once she had the baby in her arms, Kate spent a moment or two staring fondly down at her niece. Then she glanced up and caught her brother's eye. "Jack's home."

Cord's dark brows drew together. "Since when?"

"Since now. He just got in. He said he finally got my letter about Dad and he came as soon as he could." Becky had finished. She pulled off the nipple. Hannah held out her hand. Kate passed her the bottle. "I ran into him down in the kitchen a few minutes ago—along with Rafe, who'd just got in himself."

Hannah found herself thinking how strange it was to live in a house so big, people came and went and half the time, you didn't even know when someone arrived, let alone when they left.

Cord asked. "How does Jack look?"

"Tired," Kate said. "And tanned. He's staying in for dinner. And so is Rafe. How about you?"

"I'll be here." Cord gave Kate the diaper that he'd taken from his shoulder.

Kate smoothed the diaper in place and raised Becky to burping position. "I thought I'd tell Emma we want to eat about seven." Becky burped. "Good girl." Kate kissed her soft temple and spoke to Cord again. "In the sunroom?" She turned her glance Hannah's way. "We avoid the dining room whenever possible. The table there seats thirty. It's like sharing a meal in a football field."

"Seven's good," Cord said. "In the sunroom."

Kate was still looking at Hannah. "Eating in your room must be getting a little old by now. Why don't you join us?"

"Oh, no." Hannah was shaking her head before Kate even finished talking. "That's all right. I—"

"Yes," Cord insisted. "Eat with us."

"No, really. Your brother just came home. I don't want to interrupt your family meal."

Kate rubbed Becky's back. "Honestly. You won't be interrupting."

"But I—"

"Stop making excuses," Cord commanded. "It's not a big deal, it's just us."

Just us. Now, why did she like the sound of that so much?

"Say yes, Hannah," Kate coaxed. "I'm catching on to Becky's schedule. She's usually napping around seven. She shouldn't be needing you then and you know it."

"I—"

"One word," said Cord. "The word is yes."

What could it hurt? It was only a meal. "All right. Yes."

"Great," said Kate. "Now take this little darling and I'll see you at dinner."

Kate passed the baby back to her brother and went out the way she had come.

Once they were alone, Cord cleared his throat. "This isn't formal, but..." He glanced, way too significantly, down at Hannah's bare feet.

"Don't you worry, Cord Stockwell," she told him pertly. "For dinner with your brothers and sister, I'm fixing to wear shoes."

The sunroom was at the front of the house. It had double-paned floor-to-ceiling windows that let in the mellow light of the fading day, but kept out the heat. Plants grew everywhere—ferns and orchids and passion flower vines, several different kinds of palms, bamboo plants—really, there were so many varieties, Hannah couldn't have named them all if she'd tried. They hung from hooks in the ceiling and stood in huge pots before the wall of windows. In the corners, she saw shy mimosas and umbrella-shaped Norfolk Island pines. The furniture was old and comfortable, with lots of big, soft pillows and tables stacked with books. Hannah found it no surprise at all that the Stockwells liked to gather here.

Dinner was served at a round table not far from the windows.

Kate introduced Hannah to Jack. He was a big man, like his brothers, with the same blue eyes and deep brown hair—and a certain world-weariness the other two didn't share. Jack was vague about where he'd been recently, but he told them he was home to stay for a while.

"You've been in to see Daddy?" Kate asked, just carefully enough that Hannah would have known there was something wrong between Jack and his father even if Cord hadn't already told her as much.

"I've seen him," Jack replied. The words were flat as the back of a hard hand. "He was thrilled at the sight of me. As usual." His tone said it all; Caine Stockwell had been anything *but* thrilled to see his oldest son. "He looks bad. Is he still getting chemo?"

Cord shook his head. "They decided it was time to stop it. It's not going to save him at this point, anyway. And he's sick enough as it is, with the cancer itself—not to mention the combination of meds he's on."

"How long do they give him?"

"Depends on which of them you ask. Not more than a few months, at the outside."

Kate put her hand on her oldest brother's arm. "It's so good to have you home."

Jack smiled at her, his natural reserve falling away for a moment, so Hannah could see the frank affection he felt for his only sister. "Good to *be* home—" he chuckled, the sound lacking in real humor "—at least, it's *mostly* good to be home." He looked at Cord. "Maybe we should think about moving him to the hospital."

"Good luck getting him out of that room of his. He's sworn to die in this house."

"But if he'd be better off in the hospital, then he ought to be there, whether he likes it or not."

Cord shook his head. "He's got the best care money can buy. And he's got it round-the-clock. His doctors actually approve of his staying here. There's not much more they could do for him in a hospital than what can be done for him here. And at least he's where he wants to be."

Kate said, "Cord, you'd better bring Jack up to speed

on the things Dad's been telling you lately." She sent an apologetic glance in Hannah's direction. "And then we can move on to more pleasant subjects."

Cord's hand brushed Hannah's knee under the table. It was a very light, very brief touch. And the terrifying thing about it was that it felt absolutely natural for him to touch her like that.

"Don't worry about Hannah," he said. "She's heard it all already. And she has a theory or two of her own."

Oh, what was the matter with that man? A moment ago, she'd felt comfortably invisible, just sitting there listening to the others, enjoying her prime rib. But then Cord had to go and brush her knee like it was something he did all the time. And now, after what he'd just said, the others had decided she deserved their undivided attention. Three sets of blue eyes stared at her expectantly.

"What theories?" Jack asked coolly.

Hannah forced down the bite of tender beef she had just made the mistake of sticking into her mouth. It felt like a lump of sawdust as it worked its way down her throat. She knew her silly cheeks were flaming. "Uh...Cord is exaggerating. I don't have any theories. I just...expressed some doubts and made a couple of suggestions, that's all."

"Then what are your doubts?" Rafe wanted to know.

"Wait a minute," Cord said. "Before we get to Hannah's theories—"

Hannah set down her heavy silver fork with the fancy *S* engraved on the handle. "I told you, Cord Stockwell. I don't *have* any—"

"All right, all right. Before we get to your doubts. Is that right? Doubts? And suggestions?" He laid his hand over hers.

She froze. And she wanted to feel angry. But somehow,

she wasn't mad at all. Because, like his brushing touch a moment before, his hand on hers felt absolutely right.

"Well?" he prompted.

"Yes," she said reluctantly. "Doubts and suggestions. That's right."

He gave her hand a quick, warm squeeze—and released it. Hannah made herself pick up her fork again and eat more of the delicious meal as Cord brought Jack up to speed on the strange things Caine Stockwell had been raving about in recent weeks.

"I don't know," Jack said, once Cord was done. "It could all be nothing more than a sick old man's drug-induced delusions."

Cord sipped red wine from a crystal wineglass. "That's what I kept telling myself. But then Hannah started asking me questions. And now, I realize that all we ever had, when it came to the boating accident, was what the old man told us. I don't remember it, myself." He looked from Jack to Kate and then to Rafe. "How about you?"

All three shook their heads.

Cord said, "I never saw any newspaper clippings about the drownings. You'd think something like that would have been in both the *Morning News* and the *Grandview Gazette,* at least. And nobody ever talked about it, you know? None of dad's old cronies, none of the servants. No one. Maybe I'm getting as paranoid as the old man, but lately, it's started to seem to me as if he might have ordered them all to keep their mouths shut."

"You think so?" Kate's blue eyes were wide.

Cord shrugged. "Hell. You know our father. With him, anything is possible."

"The thing about the land deal is pretty strange, too," Rafe said. "I remember all the old stories Dad used to tell about the Johnsons—how they had it all way back when. And then, by the thirties, they were dirt poor and working for us. What Dad never said was *how* they managed to lose what they had. To think that maybe Great-Grandfather Caine stole it from them is pretty damn ugly.''

Cord sipped more wine. ''The question is, should we be looking into all this?'' He sent Hannah a conspiratorial glance, one that made her skin feel warm and her silly stomach jittery. ''Hannah suggested we could hire a private investigator to look into both the drownings and the land deal. The idea has merit, I think. Brett Larson has the biggest detective agency in the area. We could—''

''Wait,'' Kate said, her voice gone tight and her face suddenly just a little too pale. ''We don't really need to call Brett at this point, do we?''

Her brothers shared a look. Then Jack said, ''Kate's right. I'm here. And I've got the time at the moment. I'll do a little nosing around.''

''Let's start with the drownings,'' Cord suggested.

''Fine. I'll find out what I can about what happened out on Stockwell Pond twenty-nine years ago.''

''What went on between Kate and the man named Brett Larson?'' Hannah asked Cord at eleven-fifteen that night, after Becky had been fed, changed and put to bed—hopefully for the last time that day.

''You don't miss much, do you?''

''She looked a little pale, when the name came up.'' Hannah kept her voice low, in order not to disturb the sleeping baby.

''We grew up with Brett. His mother worked for a judge who owns the estate that borders this one.''

They stepped into the playroom. Hannah pulled the

door shut behind them. "But what happened between Kate and Brett?"

"They were engaged, at one time."

"And?"

"It didn't work out. She married someone else."

"And the marriage?"

"It didn't last."

Hannah pulled one of the sturdy child-size chairs out from under the matching child-size table. Scooping her skirt close to her legs, she sat. "So do you think she's still pining for Brett Larson?"

Cord was standing over her, looking down, a half smile playing at the edges of his mouth. "My sister is a Stockwell. A Stockwell does not pine."

She slid off her shoes and wiggled her toes. "Oh, sorry. I suppose I should have known that. And you didn't really answer my question."

"You'll have to ask Kate."

"Now, why did I know you'd say that?"

"You're a nosy woman, Hannah." Somehow, he made it sound like a compliment.

She beamed up at him. "Why, thank you." She gestured at his feet and let him have all the twang she could muster. "Kick your shoes off. Sit a spell."

He surprised her by doing just that, shucking off those fine Italian shoes of his and plunking himself right down on the rug at her feet.

They talked for over an hour—about Caine and the mysteries behind all the strange things he had said.

And about Jack. "He didn't say it in so many words," Cord told her, "but he's here because of our father."

"Because he's so ill?"

"Because he's dying. In spite of the way Caine's always treated him, Jack will stick by him till the end."

"Is that another Stockwell trait? Loyalty?"

"Absolutely."

He was looking a little grim. Hannah cast about for some way to lighten the mood. "Look at it this way. Maybe you'll get to play a little pinochle while he's home."

He leaned close enough that his shoulder brushed against her knee. Little prickles of sensation radiated out from the point of contact. "Only if you'll be my partner."

She should have moved her leg away, so he couldn't brush against it again. But she didn't. "It's a game for four. If we're partners, then someone will be left out."

"We'll play on a night when one of the others isn't around."

She heard herself murmuring, "I'd like that," as a voice in the back of her mind asked her what in the world she thought she was up to, agreeing to partner with Cord Stockwell in double deck pinochle, letting him brush his shoulder against her leg and not doing a thing to prevent it from happening again.

It did happen again. And again.

And each time it happened, she smiled and pretended she didn't even notice, while every nerve she had was fizzing and popping like the bubbles in a sparkling glass of champagne.

It was after midnight when he left. He scooped up those expensive shoes of his and gathered his strong legs under him, rising to his feet in one fluid motion. "I'll see you first thing tomorrow."

She jumped to her feet and trailed behind him to the door. And then, shamelessly, she leaned there in the doorway and watched him walk away toward his bedroom at the end of the hall. He had the broadest, strongest looking shoulders. And a woman could go weak in the knees looking at that tight rear end of his. When he reached his door, he turned and saw her watching.

She felt the color rise in her cheeks, but she didn't turn away. They stared at each other for several lovely seconds. And then, at last, he turned the doorknob and disappeared into his room.

"Come down to dinner again tonight," he said the next day during their stroll on the grounds.

She was utterly shameless. She didn't even hesitate. She said, "Thank you very much, I believe that I will."

He brought Jack to meet Becky in the afternoon, and that evening in the sunroom, Jack reported that he'd spent several hours at the library, studying back issues of the *Morning News*. "The way I remember it," Jack said. "Caine always claimed the accident happened on the Fourth of July."

"Yeah," said Cord. "That's how I remember it, too. Fourth of July, twenty-nine years ago next month."

"Me, too," Kate said. And Rafe nodded as well.

Jack continued, "So I checked the *Morning News* for the fifth of July, twenty-nine years ago. Nothing. I broadened my search. By the time I was through, I'd checked all of May, June, July and August."

"And?" Kate asked.

"Nothing. Not about any accident, anyway. And it's pretty bizarre, because there's a write-up in the Guide section about the Independence Day party."

Hannah cast a puzzled glance at Cord. He explained, "It's an annual event, every year for the past fifty years or so, here at the mansion. A big Fourth of July party. It lasts from the afternoon into the evening. We serve Texas-style barbecue and just about everything else known to man, from pâté de foie gras to hearts of palm. People use the pool and the tennis courts. And there's dancing. We bring in a dance floor and set it up out on the east lawn. And then, after dark, we have fireworks over the pond. That's more of a challenge every year, wrangling the permits to put on the fireworks show. We usually invite about three hundred guests.''

"Dahling, everybody who's *anybody* is there," Kate told Hannah playfully.

Jack said, ''There's a lot in that article about what a great party it was that year. Not a single mention of a double drowning, however.''

Rafe drank from his water goblet. ''Did you check the *Gazette,* too?''

Jack nodded. ''Nothing. And you know, it's got me thinking back. None of us remember that day. And I can understand why the rest of you don't. Kate wasn't much more than a baby.'' He looked at Cord. ''You and Rafe were only four. But I was six. Of all of us, I should remember, shouldn't I? If my mother drowned…and during the biggest party of the year? But I don't. I don't even remember the party, really. All the Independence Day parties tend to blur together in my mind.''

Kate suggested gently, ''It could be you're blocking it.''

Jack looked at his sister straight on. ''I'm not. I know what I remember—and I don't remember that Madelyn drowned.''

''If she *did* drown,'' said Rafe. ''It's beginning to look doubtful.''

For a moment, no one spoke as they all pondered the ramifications, should it turn out that Madelyn and Brandon Stockwell hadn't died in the boating accident, after all. Hannah did find it strange that the four Stockwell siblings had never questioned all this before. But then again, maybe none of them had been ready to seek the truth until now.

"Give me a week or so on this," Jack said at last. "I'll get a hold of some of Dad's old buddies, set up a few meetings with them and see what I can get out of them."

"And then what do we do?" Kate wanted to know.

"Depends on what I find out." Jack turned to Cord. "Next time the old man decides to confide in you, see if you can get us a few specifics to work with."

Cord shook his head. "He's never anywhere approaching lucid when he starts in with me."

"Just get whatever you can. Names of anyone who was there when they drowned, *if* they drowned. Or, if he starts in on how they ran away, then try to find out where they went. Any little detail could be the clue we need."

Cord said he'd do his best.

The next night, Sunday, Cord insisted that Hannah join them for dinner again. And he didn't have to insist very hard. Hannah was starting to look forward to her evenings in the sunroom. She loved Becky with all of her heart, but it was nice, once a day, to enjoy a civilized meal with a group of people who could actually answer back when she asked a question.

That night, Rafe wasn't there. Kate said he'd told her he'd be gone for a few days. He had to chase some desperado down into Mexico and bring him back to the U.S. to stand trial.

Cord said, "So we're a foursome. Perfect for pinochle."

Jack turned to Hannah, anticipation on his rugged face. "You don't…"

She nodded. "You bet I do."

So it was Jack and Kate versus Cord and Hannah.

They played for two hours, ruthlessly, shouting at each

PLAY SILHOUETTE'S
LUCKY HEARTS
GAME

AND YOU GET

♦ **FREE BOOKS!**
♦ **A FREE GIFT!**
♦ **YOURS TO KEEP!**

TURN THE PAGE AND DEAL YOURSELF IN...

Play **LUCKY HEARTS** for this...

exciting FREE gift!
This surprise mystery gift could be yours free

when you play **LUCKY HEARTS!**
...then continue your lucky streak with a sweetheart of a deal!

1. Play Lucky Hearts as instructed on the opposite page.

2. Send back this card and you'll receive 2 brand-new Silhouette Special Edition® novels. These books have a cover price of $4.50 each in the U.S. and $5.25 each in Canada, bu they are yours to keep absolutely free.

3. There's no catch! You're under no obligation to buy anything. We charge nothing— ZERO—for your first shipment. And you don't have to make any minimum number of purchases—not even one!

4. The fact is thousands of readers enjoy receiving their books by mail from the Silhouette Reader Service™. They enjoy the convenience of home delivery...they like getting the best new novels at discount prices, BEFORE they're available in stores...and they love their *Heart to Heart* subscriber newsletter featuring author news, horoscopes, recipes, book reviews and much more!

5. We hope that after receiving your free books you'll want to remain a subscriber. But the choice is yours—to continue or cancel, any time at all! So why not take us up on our invitation, with no risk of any kind. You'll be glad you did!

Visit us online at
www.eHarlequin.com

The Silhouette Reader Service™—Here's how it works:

Accepting your 2 free books and gift places you under no obligation to buy anything. You may keep the books and gift and return the shipping statement marked "cancel." If you do not cancel, about a month later we'll send you 6 additional novels and bill you just $3.80 each in the U.S., or $4.21 each in Canada, plus 25¢ shipping & handling per book and applicable taxes if any.* That's the complete price and — compared to cover prices of $4.50 each in the U.S. and $5.25 each in Canada — it's quite a bargain! You may cancel at any time, but if you choose to continue, every month we'll send you 6 more books, which you may either purchase at the discount price or return to us and cancel your subscription.

*Terms and prices subject to change without notice. Sales tax applicable in N.Y. Canadian residents will be charged applicable provincial taxes and GST.

other at the hint of a renege, slapping their cards down in hot defiance, or sitting absolutely silent, all four of them fiercely counting cards, trying to figure out who was likely to have what.

At a little after eleven, Becky started to fuss, her whimpers reaching them over the monitor Hannah had brought downstairs with her.

"Baby break," said Cord. At that point, he and Hannah were a hundred points behind. "Give us half an hour. We'll be back."

"You're done for," Jack taunted. "Give it up now."

"No way. We're going to win this thing. Come on, Hannah, let's get Becky fed and back to bed."

They went up the wide stairs side by side. Hannah warmed the bottle, and Cord fed and changed Becky. They were back down in the sunroom in twenty minutes flat.

The game continued until 2:00 a.m., when Hannah and Cord finally won.

Jack wanted a rematch. "I know, I know. Tomorrow's Monday and all you civilians have to work. But next Friday night, what do you say?"

Cord didn't hesitate. "I say, you're on."

Hannah and Kate chorused their agreement.

It wasn't until near dawn that morning, as she lay in her bed in the nanny's room, staring up at the ceiling and wondering what was happening to her, that Hannah realized she couldn't possibly play pinochle with Cord and Kate and Jack next Friday night. By next Friday night, she would be gone. She'd have hired her replacement and she'd be back in her own house where she belonged.

The idea filled her with misery.

So she decided she wouldn't think about it. She'd take care of Becky, conduct the necessary interviews and enjoy Cord's company. And she wouldn't deal with the pain of leaving until the time for leaving came.

Chapter Ten

On Monday, there were four nanny candidates to see. On Tuesday, there were six. And on Wednesday, five.

None of them were right.

Hannah was beginning to wonder if she'd ever find the woman she sought.

But she wasn't wondering all that hard. And neither was Cord, apparently. Though they talked all the time, at length, on any number of diverse topics, they never discussed the nanny problem. He hadn't asked in days how she was doing with her search. And she never volunteered any information about it. It just seemed safer somehow, to stay away from that particular subject.

All three nights—Monday, Tuesday and Wednesday—Hannah ate dinner in the sunroom with Cord and Kate and Jack. Rafe was still off in Mexico, or wherever the hunt for the latest fugitive from justice had taken him. On Wednesday, Jack said he'd met with a couple of Caine's past associates. Both had proved unforthcoming on the subject of Madelyn and Brandon and what had really happened to them. So he'd paid a visit to the county courthouse. He had found no records of Brandon's and Madelyn's deaths.

"While I was there," he said, "I tried to check into the other thing—the land deal?"

Cord picked up on the operative word. "You tried?"

"Right. The Grandview County Courthouse burned to the ground back in 1912. Everything, including all deeds, tax and assessment records, burned with it."

"Great," Cord said darkly.

"I'll keep checking around."

"Whatever you can find out…"

Jack looked wearier than usual. "So far, unfortunately, it's not a hell of a lot."

Thursday morning, Cord came to the nursery at seven, as he always did now. He fed and changed Becky and then he told Hannah that he was flying down to Houston for the day.

Gently he laid his daughter in her crib. She looked up at him, waving her arms and legs, making happy sounds. "I've got a dinner meeting," he added, still bent over the crib. "So I'll just stay over and fly back tomorrow morning."

Somehow, Hannah's poor heart had become a lead ball, a dead weight in her chest. Tomorrow would be Friday. Lord. Friday already. Today or tomorrow, she would have to find the new nanny. She intended to return to her apartment by tomorrow night, to give herself the weekend to get back to her old routines. And Monday morning was supposed to find her right where she really belonged— behind her desk at Child Protective Services.

In the meantime, though, she'd allowed herself to look forward to every minute she could spend with Cord. And now, fool that she was, she felt cheated that he'd be gone the whole day and part of tomorrow. She knew she had no right at all to such feelings. But that didn't do a thing to stop her from having them.

Just as she was telling herself to buck up and get real about all this, he glanced up from the crib and right into her eyes. "Come with me."

Her silly heart stopped being a lead ball and became a hot air balloon. It floated, utterly weightless, high in her chest. Yes. Of course. Why hadn't she thought of that? She and Becky could go with him.

She stared at him, thinking that she would go anywhere with him—to Houston, to Timbuktu, to the ends of the earth.

He straightened from the crib. "Pack light. It's only overnight. No need to bring the whole closet—how are you in small planes?"

She blinked. "Small planes?"

"Stockwell International owns several airplanes. We'll be taking the Cessna this time. But really, it's nothing to worry about. The cabin is pressurized. Becky should do fine."

She stared at his beautiful mouth, thinking that she wanted, more than anything, to go with him.

But she couldn't.

"Cord..."

His eyes narrowed. "I don't like that way you said that."

"Cord, I am sorry. I'd love to go with you, honestly. But I—"

"No buts. Nothing's stopping you. You pack the

clothes. You get on the plane. In no time at all, you and Becky are in Houston—with me.''

''No. Really, I—''

''Really you, what?'' His expression had hardened.

''It's not a good idea.''

He swore, with feeling. ''It's a *great* idea. It's the *only* idea.'' He took a step toward her. ''Start packing.''

The look in his eyes sent a delicious, forbidden thrill coursing through her. Her hot air balloon of a heart pumped higher, harder. ''No. Sincerely, I just can't.''

''You want to go. I can see it in your eyes.''

''What I want isn't the issue.''

''It sure as hell is. What's stopping you?'' Before she could answer, he answered for her. ''Nothing. Nothing at all.''

''But—''

''Nothing,'' he repeated, and took another step toward her. ''Just say yes.''

''No.'' She backed up two steps, her bare feet whispering over the starry rug. ''Cord. Please. Stop this. I really can't. I've got interviews today.''

''Cancel them.'' He kept coming.

And she kept backing up. ''No. No, I'm not going to do that.'' Her feet reached smooth wood floor. ''I'm...'' She hated to say it, but he was forcing her to. ''I'm running out of time, Cord. They're expecting me at work on Monday.''

''You *are* working. You're working for me.''

She backed through the door to the playroom. And he came right with her.

''Cord, please, I only have a few more days. I can't afford to go flying off to Houston.''

Still, he came toward her. ''You can afford it. I'll make

it more than worth your while. How much do you want? Name your price."

She put out a hand. "Stop."

He froze, and so did she, in the middle of the playroom. There was a distance of about four feet between them. In that space, the air seemed to shimmer with tension—with heat.

Hannah realized she was holding her breath. She let it out with great care. "It's not the money. You know it's not."

"Then what the hell is it?"

"Cord. This...arrangement we have, it's only temporary. We can't let ourselves forget that."

"Yes, we can." His voice was low, intense. It rubbed every nerve she had, making them all stand to eager attention. "You can stay here. I don't want any other woman raising my little girl, anyway. And you don't want to leave Becky. It'll kill you to leave her."

What he didn't say hung in the thick air between them: You don't want to leave *me,* either.

She shook her head. "No. No, it will not kill me. It'll hurt. Bad. But I'll get over it."

"Damn it, you don't *have* to get over it. Forget the interviews. Admit the damn truth. You don't *want* to replace yourself."

"Please stop telling me what I want."

He dared another step.

She said it again, "Stop," in a raw whisper.

But this time he ignored her command. He took the last step that brought him right up into her face. Her helium balloon of a heart bounced even higher.

Blue eyes burned into hers. "Pack your bag and a bag for Becky. You're coming to Houston with me."

"No, Cord. I'm not. I'm sorry. I have work to do here."

He lifted both big hands.

Ka-boom, ka-boom, ka-boom went her heart.

She saw what was about to happen. It was right there, in his eyes.

He would take her by the arms and haul her against him. His mouth would come down on hers. She would taste his kiss—his *forbidden* kiss, the kiss that both of them had vowed would never take place.

And she wanted it. She wanted it with all that was in her to want.

But Cord Stockwell had more control than that. He muttered another low invective. And he dropped his arms.

He took one step back and he said, very softly, "I told you that nothing would happen between us."

Her throat felt like big fingers were squeezing it hard. "I...yes," she managed to croak. "That's what you said."

"And I meant it. Nothing is going to happen—unless you say it's what you want."

She caught her lower lip between her teeth—and then released it. "I don't think that would be a very good idea."

"So? Do it anyway."

"No."

His gaze roamed her face. "You sound certain."

"I'm positive."

His eyes were blue ice. "Then we know where we stand, at least. Don't we?"

"We do."

He said, with total lack of sincerity, "Good luck with those interviews." He arched a brow at her. "How many have there been so far?"

She had no answer ready. It wasn't as if she'd been keeping an exact tally.

"What?" he taunted. "Lost count?"

"Of course not." She glared at him as she added them up. "There have been thirty-four—no, thirty-five. Yes. Thirty-five applicants so far."

"Thirty-five. Impressive. And not one of them has been what you're looking for."

She didn't reply. It seemed much wiser, right then, to keep her mouth shut.

"It's almost starting to seem as if you're never going to find that perfect nanny, isn't it?"

"I'll find her. Don't you worry."

"Did I say I was worried?"

"Well, if you were, you don't need to be."

"Hannah, you can stay in this house as long as you want to. Take forever to find the damn nanny. It's all right with me."

"Thank you. But forever won't be necessary."

He made a low, derisive sound in his throat. "Did I say *forever?* Imagine that. It's a word I *never* use."

She folded her arms over her stomach, hurt all out of proportion by the cynicism in his tone.

It was silly to be hurt, and she knew it.

He had never lied to her, never pretended to be anything other than what he was—a man born to privilege, who had a talent for making money. A man who adored women. Lots of women, one after the other, in a never-ending chain. He'd said he didn't have it in him to be true to just one.

Still, in the time she had spent with him, teaching him how to care for his daughter, getting to know his family, hearing the stories of his childhood, Hannah had come to believe there was real goodness in him. And sometimes she knew he saw the goodness in himself.

Not right now, though.

Right now, he looked at her through calculating eyes. Right now, he was the ruthless Caine Stockwell's favorite son, a chip off the old block in every way.

The morning had barely begun, but all at once Hannah felt very tired. "I don't want to fight with you, Cord. I truly don't."

His lips pulled back from his fine, white teeth in a cruel approximation of a smile. "You call this fighting?"

"Sparring, then. Whatever. Trading insults and digs. I don't like it. Can't we just stop?"

He stared at her. His gaze seemed to burrow right down into the center of her. Then he stuck his hands into the pockets of his beautiful gray silk slacks—as if he had to, to keep himself from reaching for her.

"You're driving me crazy," he said low. The cruel smile had vanished. He was deadly serious now. "We're going to have to do something about it. One way or the other. You'd better find that nanny and go back where you're so sure you belong. Or else you'd better admit where the two of us are headed."

"I don't—"

He silenced her with a look. "Think about it. While I'm gone." Then he turned without another word and went out through the door to the hall.

Chapter Eleven

*T*hink about it, he'd said.

As if she could think of anything else.

Hannah saw five nanny candidates between nine in the morning and three in the afternoon. She tried to focus on the answers they gave to her questions, to pay close attention to the way they interacted with Becky. She needed to find the right person to take care of Becky and she needed to find that person fast.

But it was hopeless.

Her mind kept wandering off to places she had no business allowing it to go.

She kept seeing the two of them—herself and Cord—facing off in the playroom just the way they had that morning. But then everything would go haywire. Instead of stepping back, he would reach for her. She could actually feel the heat of his mouth on hers, the pressure of his hands splayed on her back, holding her so close against him. She felt herself melting, sighing, crying out as she returned his kiss...

She'd shake herself. She'd order her foolish mind back to the here and now—only to take one look at Becky and want to burst into tears.

Oh, she didn't want to leave her. It *would* be a little like dying to walk away from her.

But what was the alternative?

Cord had made that pretty clear.

She had to get out. Or she would end up in his bed.

He might be a cynic, but he was an *honest* one.

And she had to agree with him. They probably couldn't go on much longer as they were.

The attraction, at least on her part, was much too powerful.

And what good could come of a love affair between them?

Oh, she could hardly believe she was even considering it.

But she was. Lord help her, she was.

What good could come of it?

She could see none. He'd made it clear it wouldn't be anything with the word forever in it. And once it was over, she would end up just as she had seven years ago. Picking up the pieces. Trying to find a reason to go on.

At three-fifteen, after she'd thanked the fifth nanny candidate of the day and sent her on her way, the phone rang in her room. She left Becky in the baby swing and hurried to answer.

"Ms. Miller, you have a call." It was Emma Hightower. "Someone named Maya from Child Protective Services."

Maya Revere was a fellow caseworker at CPS. She'd

been helping to fill in for Hannah while she was gone. "Thanks, Mrs. Hightower."

"Just push the second button down on the right."

"Will do." Hannah punched the button. "Maya?"

"Hey." Maya put on a heavy Southern drawl. "How's it going up there at de big hay-ouse?"

"It's going okay. How are things with you?"

"You don't want to ask me that. You'll only feel guilty when you hear my answer. Anyway, I didn't call to complain."

Hannah grinned. She did like Maya, who braided bright beads into her dreadlocks and always wore a wide, friendly smile, even though, in their line of work, there wasn't always much to smile about. "What then?"

"You said you wanted me to let you know when the Stockwell letter came in from DNA Profiling."

Hannah clutched the receiver a fraction tighter. "It came?"

"Today." Which meant that a copy had probably been delivered to the mansion, as well. A copy with Cord Stockwell's name on it. The lab had been given instructions to inform both the baby's caseworker and the father in question.

"What does it say?"

"I don't know. I haven't opened it yet. Do you want me to?"

Hannah hesitated. She considered driving over there and collecting the letter to read in private.

But that was silly. Either Cord was Becky's father or he wasn't. Keeping a secret of it from Maya Revere wouldn't change the facts.

"Hannah? Girlfriend, you still there?"

"Sorry. I'm here. Please. Read it to me—just the conclusion will be fine."

"All right, then." Hannah heard paper crackling. "Let's see." Maya coughed. "It says…a 99.9 percent likelihood."

Hannah felt moisture burning in her eyes. She swallowed the sudden lump in her throat. "So. He *is* the father."

"You're surprised?"

"No." And she wasn't. A dream had died, that was all. The faint, fading hope that a miracle might occur. That somehow she would manage to adopt Becky herself.

She'd pretty much accepted that it would never happen. But the lab results brought reality into even sharper focus. Becky Lott was a Stockwell. Cord was her natural father. He had a father's irrefutable claim.

From the other room, in the wind-up baby swing where Hannah had left her, Becky started crying. The sound reminded Hannah how very much she loved the child. The lump formed again in her throat and a single tear overflowed to slide down her cheek.

She said, "Thanks, Maya."

"You okay?"

"Fine." She swiped that futile tear away. "Becky's fussing…"

"Gotta go?"

"'Fraid so."

"You'll be in on Monday, right?"

Hannah thought of Cord again, of the heat in his eyes and the hunger in his voice just before he'd walked out on her that morning.

You're driving me crazy…

We're going to have to do something about it…

"Hannah. Yoo-hoo. Are you coming in Monday or not?"

"I'll be there."

"Say that like you mean it."

"I do mean it. I'll see you Monday. And thanks. For getting that information right to me."

"Anytime."

Hannah said goodbye and went to comfort the wailing Becky.

Later, Kate dropped by. She fed Becky and played with her on the changing bureau, rattling rattles and practicing the most basic versions of peekaboo.

"Come down for dinner. Seven-thirty," Kate said before she left.

Hannah almost said no. She didn't feel much like company that evening. But Kate had become a friend—a friend who was definitely no fool. Hannah knew if she turned the invitation down she would end up having to explain why.

"I'll be there."

It was a quiet meal, just the two of them. Rafe hadn't returned from his last assignment. "And I haven't a clue where Jack's gone off to," Kate said. "But he's not here. It's just us girls."

They ended up talking jobs and movies and sharing a few childhood stories. Hannah was careful to keep the talk away from the subject of men, though she really would have liked to ask a question or two about the man named Brett Larson. But man talk, right then, was way too dangerous—even with another woman as bright and sympathetic as Kate. For Hannah, talking men could and probably would lead straight to Cord Stockwell. And the last thing she wanted was to end up crying on his sister's shoulder.

What could she tell Kate anyway?

I want your brother. I think I *love* your brother. And falling for him is probably the second most ridiculously foolish thing I've ever done in my life—no. Wait. Make that the *most* ridiculously foolish thing. I was seventeen before, and I didn't know any better. Now, I'm twenty-five, a grown woman who ought to have learned something from the whopper of a mistake she made once.

And then, of course, Kate would ask, "What mistake?"

No. It was not a good idea to start talking men with Kate.

Hannah excused herself at a little before nine. Upstairs, Becky was still sleeping, so Hannah turned on the television in her room and channel-surfed for a while. When she couldn't find a single thing that held her interest, she turned it off and tried to read.

That didn't work, either. The words blurred in front of her. Instead she saw blue eyes and a mouth she wanted to feel pressed against her own.

She kept hearing those cruel things he had said...

Did I say forever? Imagine that. It's a word I never use. And, *You call this fighting?* And worst of all, *You'd better find that nanny and go back where you're so sure you belong. Or else you'd better admit where the two of us are headed.*

Another day down. And she had *not* hired the nanny. She could easily become very disgusted with herself.

At ten-fifteen, she gave up on her book. She marked her place—only a few pages from where she'd begun an hour before—and went into the small bath off the nanny's room. She took a quick, hot shower and brushed her teeth. By ten-forty, she was dressed in her nightgown, all ready to sneak a few winks before Becky woke and wanted one more meal.

She got under the covers and switched off the lamp.

And stared at the ceiling.

The wind was up outside. She had been aware of it

before. But now, with no book or television image to distract her, she thought it seemed louder than before, hard and insistent, rushing at the thick walls of Stockwell Mansion, rattling the windows. A wild Texas wind—which wasn't a heck of a lot different from an Oklahoma wind. Both blew strong and relentlessly.

She lay there, listening to it gust and moan, watching the dim shadows play across the ceiling, waiting for Becky to wake and cry out.

But it wasn't Becky she heard, from the monitor on the windowsill.

It was a sound so soft, she might have missed it beneath the crying of the wind, had not every sense she possessed been so acutely attuned right then.

The faint creak of a door opening. Yes. She knew that was what she had heard.

There was someone in Becky's room.

The wind howled louder, a long, hard, whooshing wail of sound.

It might have been any one of the Stockwells. Or Mrs. Hightower. Or even, God forbid, an intruder.

But it wasn't.

Hannah knew who it was. She could *feel* him. He was here, in the huge house. In Becky's room. Cord Stockwell had not stayed the night in Houston, after all.

Hannah sat up in bed and started to push the covers away.

But no.

She lay back down. It was impossible. She couldn't go in there. That would only be asking for...

Exactly what she wanted.

For an endless minute or two, she remained there, flat on her back under the covers, thinking, *No, I will not go*

*in there. I will stay here. If Becky wakes, Cord can tend
to her. There is no reason for me to go in there.*

Except that *he's* in there.

And she wanted to be where he was...

In the end, she sat again. And this time she shoved the
covers to the side and swung her bare feet to the floor.

She shouldn't...

The wind gusted again, rattling the windowpanes. It had
a sad, lost sound right then, like a lonely ghost locked out
to wander in the night.

She reached for the light and then for her robe.

Chapter Twelve

Cord moved silently to the crib and stood looking down at his daughter. She lay on her back, one plump arm raised over her head, her little fist like the bud of some perfect, pink flower.

Outside, the wind howled.

He had missed her—and he had missed the infuriating woman who was sleeping in the nanny's room. Missed them both, damn it, though he'd been away from them for less than a day. So he'd wrapped up his business as fast as he could and flown himself home. His landing had been rough, with the wind so bad. But in the end, he'd touched down and taxied in safely enough. And his car was waiting for him—the Ferrari 360 Modena this time. He'd driven home way too fast. But why own a Ferrari, if you couldn't drive it good and fast?

Becky sighed, her fingers opening, then closing gently against her sweetly wrinkled little palm.

The wind howled all the louder.

Cord bent closer. Becky's eyelids were jittering. Probably dreaming. What the hell did a three-month-old baby dream of, anyway?

The simplest things, most likely. Tender arms to hold her, warm bottles full of formula, a gentle voice and a loving smile.

It occurred to him that, except for the formula, what a baby wanted wasn't a lot different than what most every other damn fool in the world wanted.

Tender arms. A gentle voice. A loving smile.

He dared to think her name: Hannah.

And just as that word whispered through his mind, the light winked on in her room.

As usual, she'd left the door to the playroom ajar, so he saw the flash of brightness at the edge of his vision. He glanced up. Yes. A sliver of golden light glowed under her door.

It all came back to him, when he saw that glow: the first night she'd come to stay in his rooms. Her light under the door. Her white gown with the virginal ruffle at the neck. His first sight of those slim, pale feet...

Damn.

He was bad off.

Lately, every thought he had seemed to lead right back around to Hannah—her smile, her laugh, her sweet Okie twang. She *was* driving him crazy. Plain out of his mind.

It wasn't supposed to have turned out like this. He should have been immune to her. He'd never been attracted to her type.

Till now.

And now? Now, he had started to see things in a whole different light. Now, he found himself thinking that it wasn't the *type* of woman that mattered, after all.

It was the woman herself.

Outside, the wind seemed to be crying. An oak branch too near the window scraped the glass—the sound like some forlorn creature scratching hopelessly in the fading chance some kind soul might take pity and open up.

He could see the shadows of her feet moving under her door. Cord stared at that door, willing it to open.

And it did.

"Cord? Is that you?"

It was the first night all over again: the white gown, that damn green robe, the pretty naked feet. Her hair was a halo around her face, dark near her head, moving outward to spun gold.

He didn't speak, just left the crib and strode toward her.

They met where they had stood that morning, in the center of the dark playroom. Met, and then hung poised there, staring way too hard into each other's eyes.

They spoke at the same time, the words breathless, and hushed.

"I didn't expect you—"

"Hannah, I'm sorry."

She put her hand to her neck, fingers touching her pale throat, her palm brushing that maddeningly innocent white ruffle. "You're...sorry?" Her soft mouth trembled.

He couldn't stop himself. He lifted a hand. Touched those lips. "The things I said, before I left—I shouldn't have said those things."

"It's all right." Her breath flowed down his palm as her mouth moved beneath his fingers. "What you said was only the truth."

His hand did what it wanted to do, sliding across the velvet softness of her cheek, moving around to cup her nape beneath the cloud of chestnut hair.

God. She was warm. And she smelled the way only she could smell. Soap and flowers and a hint of baby lotion.

He *had* to kiss her and said it aloud. "I *have* to kiss you, Hannah. Just once..."

She made a small, lost sound—of agreement, or protest? He couldn't tell which. But then she tipped her face slightly higher, offering her mouth.

He wished that could be agreement enough.

But no. She did have to say it. He had set the terms himself, promised that nothing at all would happen between them unless she admitted she wanted it, too.

"Say it, Hannah. Yes. Or no."

His heart ceased to beat as he waited for her reply.

"Yes." The one word, in a whisper.

His heart kicked to life once more.

He lowered his head and took what she offered—tenderly, carefully, with no sudden moves, letting her get to know him in this new way. He brushed his mouth over hers, nibbling a little.

Never, he thought. I will never get enough...

Was it only a moment before that his heart had ceased to beat? Impossible. Now it hammered loud and urgent, pounding in his ears.

She sighed. Her sweet breath mingled with his, her mouth trembled some more, this time beneath his.

So incredible. The taste of her...

And he couldn't hold himself back anymore. He gathered her close, slipping his free hand around her waist, his other hand cupping her nape more firmly than before.

She moaned as their bodies made contact, and she slid her own arms up over his shoulders, around his neck. He felt her, the whole slim, curvy length of her, pressed right against him as his mouth devoured hers.

He brushed his tongue along the seam where her lips

met. She moaned once more, and let him in. He tasted her all the more deeply, his hands roaming her slender back.

There were almost too many sensations for him to process—her waist between his hands, her soft breasts against his chest, her lips under his, the scent of her hair, the sweetness of her sighs...

How many women had he kissed in his lifetime, how many had he held like this? More than he should have. More than he would ever admit to. So many that the thrill of mere kissing, especially in recent years, had begun to elude him.

But not now.

Now, it was all new again.

It was the first time again.

Better than the first time. A hundred, a *thousand* times better.

It was magical, beautiful, tender and sweet.

It hurt, it was so perfect. He wanted it never, ever to stop.

It was...

Hannah.

His full arousal pressed hard at the placket of his slacks. Imagine that. From just a kiss.

But not just *any* kiss.

Hannah's kiss.

He dared to move his hands downward, to the round globes of her bottom. He cupped her and pulled her closer. She gave a cry—but a willing one, as she felt how much he wanted her.

His heart pounded harder. He sucked her tongue into his mouth, claiming it, as he pulled her into him so tight, he was probably hurting her.

But he didn't mean to hurt her. He only wanted...the

pleasure, *this* pleasure, never to stop. And she wasn't fighting him. She wasn't objecting. Her tongue in his mouth was eager, questing, driving him crazy. Wild. Out of his mind...

Outside, the wind kept crying, wailing around the brick and mortar of the massive house his grandfather had built, seeking entry it would never find.

He wanted...

All of her. To see. To touch. To taste.

To know.

Far in the back of his reeling mind, a voice began chiding, *It was only supposed to be one kiss. One kiss. That's all...*

But he didn't give a damn for that voice.

She was willing. She wanted this as much as he did...

Well, maybe not *as much.* It probably wasn't possible for her to want it *that* much.

But she did want it. Those were her arms, around his neck. It was her tongue inside his mouth.

He brought one hand between them, as he continued to hold her close with the other. He found the end of the sash that belted the green robe. He gave it a tug. The sash came away. The green robe fell open.

Letting the sash drop to the floor, he slipped his hand between the robe and the gauzy fabric of the white nightgown. She gasped into his mouth. He kissed her harder, taking that gasp into himself, his arm banding around her, pulling her up so tight she would never get away.

She returned his kiss, pressed herself against him eagerly. He brought one hand up to peel the robe away.

And the baby started crying.

Both of them froze.

Expletives echoing in his brain, he continued to hold her, close and hard, the breath scraping in and out of his lungs as if he'd just run a marathon—one he was coming to the grim realization that he was not going to win.

Becky cried louder.

Hannah pulled her mouth away from his and stared up at him wide-eyed, two spots of hectic color staining her cheeks, her mouth soft and red and very much kissed.

He resisted the urge to tangle his fingers in her hair and yank her head back again, bringing that mouth into position for another kiss.

Becky stopped crying—but only to suck in a breath and let out a long, loud, get-in-here-and-see-to-me yowl.

Fatherhood, he decided, did have its drawbacks.

Hannah pushed at his chest. He released her. She bent to scoop up the sash to her robe. She was tying it snugly in place as she hurried to deal with his child.

He remained where he was, facing the open door to Hannah's room, waiting for his arousal to subside at least a little. Becky kept wailing. The demanding cries took care of his problem. A moment later, he was able to go get the bottle ready. A few minutes after that, he took it to Hannah.

She tried to give him Becky. But he knew what would happen if he allowed that. The instant he had his daughter in his arms, Hannah would leave him. He wasn't letting that happen, so he gave her the bottle instead.

A frown creased her brow, but she didn't protest. She took the bottle and touched the nipple to Becky's howling mouth. The howling stopped.

In the silence, he was aware of the wind again, crying so sadly outside, of that lone branch scraping the windowpane.

Hannah went to the rocker and lowered herself into it. He stood by the crib and watched her feed his child.

She wouldn't meet his eyes, not at first. She rocked and

stared down at the baby. He felt she was wishing that he would just leave.

Fat chance.

Finally she looked up. He knew she was going to say something critical, something regretful. *We shouldn't have done that.* Or, *you shouldn't have kissed me.*

He was wrong.

She said, "The letter from DNA Profiling came today."

The comment was so completely out of the blue, it took him a moment to absorb it. He stared at her, wondering why she thought he would care. He already knew who Becky's father was.

"The results of that DNA test you took," she reminded him, obviously picking up on his puzzled look. "They came through. A friend at CPS called me and read me the findings. You should be getting a copy, too. Have you…did you see it already?"

He speared his fingers back through his hair. "Hannah, I just got here. I've hardly had time to check my mail."

"Well," she said. She glanced down at the baby, then met his eyes again. "It's official. You're Becky's dad." She looked as if she just might burst into tears.

He wanted to hold her, to comfort her, to tell her it was all going to be all right—whatever, exactly, *it* was. "Hell. Hannah…" He took a step toward her.

"No, don't…"

He froze.

She braced the bottle awkwardly against her breast and used her free hand to swipe at both cheeks. "I'm okay." She took the bottle in her hand again.

Suddenly he understood. "You thought, just maybe, that you could get her away from me." Should that have made him mad? Probably. But it didn't. All he felt was tenderness—and the low, insistent throb of unfulfilled desire. He said, very gently, "It wouldn't have happened, Hannah. No matter what the results of the test turned out to be."

She closed her eyes, drew in a long breath—and let it out in a rush. "Oh, please." Her pretty mouth had pursed up tight. "If she wasn't your daughter, wasn't a *Stockwell*? If she was just the baby of a woman you had slept with once, a baby fathered by another man? I don't believe you. You'd have given her up in a minute."

"No." He uttered the word with total conviction.

She actually sneered at him. "That's easy for you to say—now that there's no doubt."

He shrugged. "You're right. I always knew she was mine, from the minute I laid eyes on her. And now even *you* have to be satisfied that she is. So this is all pointless. We don't have to play 'what might have happened if?'"

She opened her mouth to reply. And then she shut it. Again, she looked down at the baby in her arms.

He said, softly, "You're angry. Because of what just happened in the other room."

She pressed her lips together and shook her head, still refusing to look at him.

"Hannah."

She swallowed and then, reluctantly, she lifted her head.

"What is it, then?"

She sighed again. "You're the last person I should tell this to."

"I don't think so. I think I'm *exactly* the person you should tell this to—whatever the hell it is."

"How can you say that, if you don't know what it is?"

"Just tell me."

"Why?"

"Because I want to know."

She gave him her sideways look, wary and measuring. "Come on."

She shook her head, but then muttered, "Oh, all right." She let it out in a rush. "It's just that...you were right, this morning. Those mean things you kept hinting at. I've been flat out lying to myself for days now, turning away one perfectly acceptable nanny applicant after another, finding reasons why none of them is ever quite good enough."

He felt his mouth trying to pull into a smile. But a smile, he decided, probably wouldn't go over too well at that moment. He kept his expression deadly serious.

She went on, "I don't want to leave this baby." She looked down at the child in her arms, a desperate look, full of love and unhappiness. "I *never* want to leave her— and God help me, I don't want to leave you, either." She said that last very low, her head bowed, her gaze on the baby.

But he heard it.

He folded his arms over his chest. It was the only way he could keep himself in place—keep himself from covering the distance between them, yanking her out of the rocker, Becky and all, and hauling her into his embrace.

She didn't want to leave him.

So they had no damn problem, after all.

Because he didn't want her to leave, either.

He wanted her in his arms.

And in his bed.

All at once, he felt totally calm. Completely sure.

He said, quietly, "She's finished."

"I know that." She still wouldn't look at him. She set the bottle on the floor beside the rocker and lifted Becky to her shoulder.

Cord waited. He would have waited a century if that had been necessary.

But it didn't take that long for Becky to complete her late-evening routine. Burping and filling her diaper—which he did not change. Not tonight. He let Hannah do it.

He was more certain of her than he'd ever dared to be till now. But once she put his baby in his arms, she could still make one last-ditch attempt at escape.

Damned if he would give her the opportunity.

So he waited. Hannah avoided looking at him, as she took Becky back to the rocker and sat down again. She rocked the baby. The wind moaned, died away, then moaned anew. Cord remained by the crib. He watched his daughter's dark eyelashes flutter down.

Finally he whispered, "She's sound asleep."

Hannah said nothing. Carefully she rose. He stepped aside enough that she could put his daughter in her bed. And then, for a moment, she stood, staring down at the sleeping child, just as he had done, earlier, when he first got home.

"She's so beautiful," Hannah whispered.

He made a low sound of agreement.

At last, she looked up. They stared at each other, heat and need seeming to arc in the air between them.

"Excuse me." She slid around him.

He followed her into the playroom, where she went to the little sink in the kitchen area and washed her hands. Once she'd turned off the taps, she pulled a paper towel from the wall dispenser. She took way too long to dry.

But finally, she couldn't stretch the simple task out for another second. She tossed the damp towel into the wastebasket under the sink.

They faced each other. He reached out and ran his finger along the smooth line of her jaw. She made a small sound, very close to a whimper, and caught her lower lip between her white teeth.

He tipped up her chin. "Where's the receiver?"

She frowned.

He prompted, "The receiver, to the baby monitor?"

She gulped. He tracked the movement of her throat with the back of his index finger. She shuddered as he stroked her.

"Is it in your room?"

"Yes. In my room."

"Go get it."

"I don't—"

"You do."

"Cord, we—"

He put his palm against her mouth. "Just get the receiver." And he waited, watching her wide, wounded eyes.

In the end, she nodded.

He dropped his hand away. She turned and padded through the open door to her room. A moment later, she was walking back toward him with the receiver in her hand.

"What now?" she said.

He took her other hand and led her out into the hall.

Chapter Thirteen

Hannah's bare feet whispered along the fancy Oriental runner in the hallway as Cord led her along. Her pulse pounded hard in her ears.

She could stop this, she thought. She could pull away. She could say no...

But she said nothing. Her heart raced and her feet followed where he led her.

To his room, at the end of the corridor.

When they got there, he turned the brass handle and pushed open the heavy door.

He stepped over the threshold and she went right along. He shut the door behind them and turned the lock beneath the handle.

In its prime location at the end of the upper hall, the big room had windows on both the north and south walls. The curtains all stood open, so that, with the lights off, everything seemed bathed in a silver glow from the lamps on the grounds below—and from the stars and the nearly full moon.

There was a large sitting area, with a full bar, comfortable chairs and a beautiful sofa upholstered in satin; it seemed to glow in the silvery light from outside. And at the other end of the room, on the westernmost wall, Hannah saw a king-size sleigh bed, head and footboard carved of some kind of beautiful burled wood. A heavy chest waited at the foot of the bed. There were bureaus and side tables, each of fine, rich old wood. The walls were hung with the kinds of pictures a man might choose—prints of bridges and airplanes, old photographs and a few framed documents. Over the full-sized stone fireplace loomed a huge oil of a sailing ship on a stormy sea. And there were flowers, fresh-cut ones, on the low tables and gracing two of the bureaus. Emma Hightower saw to it that there were fresh flowers everywhere in Stockwell Mansion—at least in the rooms that Hannah had visited.

Cord turned a dial. Two lamps, one on either side of the bed, came on, creating a warm golden glow.

He took the baby monitor from her and set it on a low table near the door. "Come with me." He pulled on her hand again. She followed automatically, across the rug that felt like velvet beneath her feet.

At the side of the beautiful bed, he released her hand. And he stepped away.

"That first night you stayed here." His voice was low and hungry and rough. "I...imagined you. In exactly this nightgown—minus the robe."

She couldn't quite believe that. That first night, they hadn't even *liked* each other. "You...imagined me?"

He nodded. "And then I knocked on your door and there you were, wearing *almost* what I'd imagined.

Shocked the hell out of me.'' His gaze scanned her face. ''Take off the damn robe, Hannah.''

She opened her mouth, but then didn't know what to say.

''Please,'' he whispered. ''Untie the sash.''

Her fingers moved to obey. Just one little tug, and the sash slithered free.

''Drop it.''

She did.

''Now, the robe. No—don't move. Stay right there, with the light behind you.''

She gathered the facings and pushed the robe off of her shoulders.

''Let it fall to the floor.''

She straightened her arms. The robe slid away.

Cord stared at her. She knew he could see right through her white nightgown.

He said, ''Exactly.'' The word had a thousand meanings, every one of them sexual. The look in his eyes sent a hot shiver through her, caused a meltdown in her midsection.

Oh, my. They shouldn't be doing this. She'd regret it come morning—but as long as they *were* doing it, she'd darn well better enjoy it. She let her lips curve into a naughty smile. ''Cord Stockwell, shame on you.''

He laughed, a low, very suggestive kind of laugh. And then he was reaching for her, pulling her close. His mouth was on hers, stealing her breath.

He kissed her slowly, lazily, taking his sweet time about it. And while he kissed her, he began to get rid of his clothes.

He was very good at that—kissing her senseless and undressing himself at the same time. He made her help him, stroking her mouth with his tongue, teasing her lips between his teeth, as he guided her hands—to his tie, to his diamond cuff links.

He took them from her, the cuff links, once she pulled them from their holes. She heard him drop them on the nightstand. And then he caught her hands again and guided them to the buttons of his beautiful silk shirt. One by one, she slid those buttons from their holes. When she undid the final button, his hands were waiting—to guide hers upward, to his shoulders, where he indicated he wanted her to push the shirt off and away.

She did what he wanted.

The shirt landed at their feet.

His naked chest confronted her, so warm and broad and hard with muscle. Crisp dark hair grew across his pectorals and down the middle of his tight belly in a silky, tempting line. Hannah laid a hand on either side of his chest, feeling the power of him, the heat of him—and his heartbeat, too, so strong and steady.

He caught her hands again, first holding them tight in his as he kicked off his shoes. And then, a moment later, guiding them downward.

Her fingers surprised her. They knew exactly what to do.

She unhooked the hooks and took the zipper down. She was a little shy of actually touching him, there, so intimately, but once or twice her fingers did brush him in passing. He gasped, both times—and so did she—as she peeled open the plackets and guided the fine slacks down over his hips and his powerful thighs.

The slacks dropped around his ankles. He sat, on the edge of the bed, pulling her down with him, his mouth still holding hers. He kicked the slacks away and managed, with incredible dexterity, to shuck off his socks.

Hannah pulled away. She stared at him. All he had left

was a pair of midnight-blue silk boxer shorts. He chuckled—probably at the look of pure surprise on her face—and he slid his hand around her nape again to bring her mouth to his once more.

Another kiss.

Oh, what the man could do with his lips and his tongue. His fingers started working at the row of buttons down the front of her nightgown. They worked fast. She felt the air—and his hand—slipping in. He cupped her breast. And he moaned into her mouth.

Hannah moaned right back as he rolled her nipple between his thumb and forefinger and then spread his hand, to cup her again. The sensation was so lovely. It made her feel weak and hot and wonderful. Arousal spiraled through her, finding its way down into her very center, stoking the need there, turning warmth to flame.

They were sitting side by side, kissing, as he caressed her. But then, all at once, he was urging her to stand again. He stood, too, kissing her all the way upright. And then he put his hands on her hips. She knew what he meant to do—pull up her gown and toss it away.

She stiffened as it came to her: when he did that, he would see—

She sucked in a breath.

No. It had been years. And the marks had never been that obvious to begin with. Surely they'd faded enough that he wouldn't notice.

And even if he did notice, so what? What was he going to say about them?

Hannah, how did you get these stretch marks?

Hardly. Cord Stockwell knew all about seduction. He would have learned a long time ago never to make an issue of a woman's physical imperfections.

"Hannah?" His eyes probed hers. "What's wrong?"

She licked her lips. "Nothing."

He looked wary now. "I don't believe you. There's something."

"There's nothing."

He frowned. "Is this your first time?"

Somehow, she restrained the sharp cry of frantic laughter that tried to burst from her throat. He assumed her hesitation stemmed from innocence.

Just the opposite was true.

"No," she said. "It's not my first time."

His frowned deepened. "Well, then. What's wrong?"

She put her hands on his shoulders and rose on tiptoe to brush his mouth with hers. "Nothing," she lied again. "Nothing at all..." Another problem occurred to her. "I...well, I'm not on the Pill or anything."

"It's all right. I can take care of it."

"Oh," she said, rather breathlessly, thinking that she should have known she didn't need to worry on that score. The man knew what he was doing. Of course, he'd have protection. He might have messed up once with Becky's mother, but he couldn't afford to have every affair result in a bouncing bundle of joy.

He wrapped his big arms around her, bringing her close to him again, deepening the kiss that she had begun.

And when he put his hands on her hips that time and began to gather the fabric of her gown in his fists, she did not stiffen or try to push him away. She just lifted her arms. He swept the nightgown up over her head.

And then, there she was. Naked before him. He looked at her with heat and hunger. If he noticed the stretch marks, he didn't seem to care. He tossed her nightgown over a chair and took her by the hand.

"Come here..." He pulled her onto the bed.

Then he buried his fingers in her hair and, kneeling with

her in the center of the huge mattress, he kissed her some more, kissed her so long, her lips ached.

A delicious ache.

All of her ached. Her whole body throbbed, with wonder, with yearning, with sweet, hot desire. He grasped her shoulders. And he guided her down, so she lay on her back, resting on the fat pillows at the head of the bed. He began to caress her in earnest, those incredible hands of his trailing down over her body, lingering for a time on her breasts, her belly, the patch of soft curls at the juncture of her thighs.

His mouth followed his hands.

Hannah lost herself in the feel of that mouth on her body, in the tender, insistent touch of those hands. She cried out, repeatedly, and she opened for him when he urged her to. She gasped and she moaned as his hands had their way with her—and, minutes later, his mouth as well. She grabbed his dark head and shamelessly pressed herself against him, pleading with him not to stop.

He didn't. The wonderful, liquid pulsing began, spreading from the point where his mouth was loving her, outward, all through her, hot and wet and wonderful: a river of fire.

She cried out again, louder than before. And then, with a final sigh, she went lax.

He waited, his incredible mouth still pressed to her most private place, absorbing the aftershocks as they quivered through her. Slowly she opened her eyes.

He lifted his head then, and he looked at her, his gaze deep and dark as the heart of midnight, his mouth swollen with what he'd been doing to her. Her breath snagged in her throat as he began kissing his way back up her body.

She whispered his name.

And he muttered, "Hannah..."

And then he was reaching for the nightstand drawer.

She couldn't believe her boldness. She helped him to slide the thing on. And she reveled in the way he groaned at her touch.

He positioned himself on top of her, most of his weight on his powerful arms. Slowly he pressed in. Her body gave easily, primed by the pleasure he had just given her. She reached up, tried to pull him close.

He resisted at first. He looked into her eyes as he filled her. Never, ever, had anyone looked at her that way, a look that seared a path right down into her very soul. She wrapped her legs around his hard hips and she urged him again to come down to her. Still, he held himself away. He shook his dark head, as if clearing it, and he captured her gaze again.

"No," he whispered on a hard breath. "I want to see you…"

"Please…"

"Don't…"

"Please, Cord…"

He swore. And he let his arms relax. She gathered him to her. He tangled his fingers her hair.

And he kissed her, his lips claiming hers as, below, he was moving inside her. She couldn't get close enough—that was impossible. But no one would ever be able to say she hadn't tried. She pressed her hands hard to his powerful back and she held him so very tightly with her legs.

About then it began to seem as if they really did share one body. And one heart.

It was beating, that heart, so hard and insistently. She shared her breath with him and he gave it right back to her, their mated bodies rising and falling, now frantic and needful, now so slow and deep it hardly seemed they were moving at all.

He stroked her hair, his mouth on hers in a kiss that felt like eternity itself, a kiss that had no beginning—and that would never end.

He freed his hands from the wild tangle of her hair. His fingers skimmed down her body, striking sparks where they touched. He found her hips, cupped them and lifted them, so that the impossible happened—he surged in deeper still.

She moaned—or he did. It didn't matter. It was all the same. *They* were the same: one body, one soul, one never-ending kiss.

She clutched him close, his body so hot, slick with the sweat of their loving, the two of them sliding together, perfectly connected, complete.

And then it happened.

The world burst apart, shooting out in a shower of light and heat, hitting the top of the universe, hovering there on a long, drawn-out sigh, then drifting down, bright sparks in the night, flickering out slowly, until there was nothing but velvety darkness—and the sad insistent wailing of the wind outside.

For a time, they just lay there, holding each other close, the sweat cooling on their skin. Eventually, though, Cord stirred.

Hannah protested with a sigh. "Don't move. Please…"

But he rolled them both, so they lay on their sides facing each other. And he ran his hand down the bumps of her spine. It felt as if he was learning the shape of each one. "I want a bath. A bubbly one. With you…"

A bath.

That sounded kind of nice.

In fact, it sounded *very* nice.

But then again, maybe not. They were, after all, both naked. It seemed nothing short of natural to be naked, holding each other close, here on Cord's bed. But to get up and stroll around his room in her birthday suit?

Uh-uh. She didn't think so. She burrowed in closer to him, hoping that just maybe, they could stay that way forever...

He put his finger under her chin and made her look at him. "Are you okay?"

He looked so honestly concerned for her comfort and well-being, it wasn't hard at all to say, "We are just so *naked*."

He chuckled. "That we are."

She suggested sheepishly, "Maybe if I had my robe..."

A teasing light danced in his eyes. "Ms. Miller, it's not customary to bathe in your robe."

"I didn't say I wanted to take a bath in it—I just need it to get me from here to the bathtub."

He ran his thumb across her lower lip. And then he bent close and kissed the place he had just touched. "No, you don't. You're beautiful naked. You don't need any damn robe."

Beautiful. Cord Stockwell had called her beautiful. The compliment delighted her.

Oh, she was such a dizzy fool...

"Well, thank you very much," she said tartly. "But I still would like my robe."

"You don't need it."

"Cord."

"What?"

"Without that robe, I don't leave this bed."

"Ever?"

"Now, you stop it. You know what I mean."

He studied her face for a moment, then gave her another quick kiss. "Tell you what. You stay here. I'll get the water running and be right back."

He didn't even wait for her answer, just rolled away from her and off the side of the bed. She shut her eyes and curled into a ball, wrapping her arms around herself, protecting the modesty she really didn't have anymore, considering all the naughty things they had recently been doing.

"Hannah."

She opened one eye—just barely, in a squint.

"Here." He was standing by the bed, buck naked, holding out her robe. Even through one squinting eye, she could see that he was quite a magnificent specimen of a man. He still wore the condom—and looked in danger of losing it.

"Uh, thank you." She snatched the robe from his hand, yanking it close to cover the most crucial areas.

He grinned at her.

"Well, go on," she told him. "Get the water ready."

Still grinning, he turned to go.

She watched him until he disappeared through the door in the corner of the room. She couldn't help herself. Watching Cord Stockwell walk away naked was something a girl couldn't let herself miss.

As soon as he was gone, she shook out her robe and stuck her arms into the sleeves, wrapping it close around her. And then she looked for the sash. It was right there, on the rug by the nightstand. She grabbed it up and tied it firmly around her waist. In the pocket, she found the big clip she'd left there earlier, after her shower. She used it to anchor her hair off her neck. Then she sat on the edge of the bed to wait for Cord to return.

It didn't take him long. He stole her breath away when

he reappeared, as naked as before—well, technically, even more so, since the condom was gone.

Beneath the rise and fall of the wind, she could hear the steady drone of water running in the other room. He took her hand. She gave it shyly. He pulled her from the bed. She went with him, hanging back only a little.

The bathroom was huge, with lots of veined black marble, on the floors and halfway up the walls, lining the counters and the double sink. Tropical plants softened all that blackness. And the huge skylight over the raised tub showed a velvety night dusted with stars. There was also a big shower stall with brass fixtures, the door to which was clear glass. A girl would need a lot of steam to protect her privacy in there.

The tub was very large—more than big enough for two—and oval in shape. The water roared from the brass taps, beating at whatever Cord had put in there to make it bubble.

The bubbles were rising, fluffy as clouds. It looked very inviting. She couldn't wait to get in there.

But first, she had to take off her robe.

Cord helped her with that, turning her to face him, pulling on the sash, tossing it away. He looked at her so tenderly as he peeled the robe from her shoulders and sent it flying to join the sash.

So there she was, naked again.

And Cord was kissing her again—a nice, long, thoroughly arousing kiss.

When he pulled away, she had to stop herself from reaching out and grabbing him back. He led her up the steps to the edge of the tub and then he paused there, beside her, with the fragrant steam rising up to surround them and the bubbles just waiting for her to sink down into them.

He touched her collarbone—traced it with his index finger. And then he let that finger trail downward, right along the center of her chest, between her breasts, where the nipples were already hard, in anticipation of his touch. She looked down, watched his big, tanned hand as it skimmed over her white skin.

His finger kept moving. It paused at her belly button and traced a circle, very slowly, around it.

Lower.

She caught her breath.

And then, very lightly, he ran the pads of his fingers along the almost invisible pale stretch marks at the base of her belly, right above the soft thatch where her thighs joined.

Hannah gasped and looked up. Their gazes met and locked.

She saw it in his eyes. He knew everything.

She drew in a breath.

No. No, of course, he didn't. He knew nothing.

He only guessed. And there was more than one way to get stretch marks, after all. Any significant weight gain—and loss—could do it.

She opened her mouth to toss off some remark about how heavy she'd been as a teenager.

But she couldn't quite make herself form the lie. Not now. Not after all that had happened between them.

The truth came out instead. "I...had a baby once."

Chapter Fourteen

"A baby who looked like Becky?" he asked very gently.

Hannah closed her eyes. "Yes. Like Becky...the dark hair, the blue eyes, the stubborn little chin..." She faltered, her throat so tight, it ached—faltered and then waited for him to say more, to press for details, for explanations.

But he said nothing. He only took her hand and kissed the back of it, his lips a tender brand against her skin.

And then he guided her down into the steaming bubbles and knelt to turn off the taps. With the water silenced, the room was way too quiet. Even the incessant wind outside seemed to have died away.

He rose to his feet again. "I'll be right back."

She felt frantic, suddenly, after what she'd just been so foolish as to reveal to him. What if he didn't come back? She'd sit here, her skin turning pruney, as all the bubbles melted away. And then, finally, she'd have to get out of the water, put on her robe and slink back to her own room.

She grabbed for him, an awkward, desperate move. "No. Wait, I—"

He knelt again, caught her hand, kissed it a second time. "Hannah. I won't be long. I promise you."

She realized she believed him. He honestly intended to come right back. She felt doubly foolish, to have reached out for him like that. With great dignity, she retrieved her hand and sank into the bubbles up to her chin. "Take your time."

He rose again, then lingered, watching her, looking way too amused. He really was pretty incredible, the way he could stand there without a stitch on, everything showing, and find *her* amusing.

"Well?" She quelled a sudden urge to cross her eyes at him.

He had the nerve to chuckle. "All right. I'm going."

She was so busy being dignified, she didn't even watch him walk away that time.

He was as good as his word. He came back just moments later, a fat crystal glass in either hand. "Two fingers of good whiskey. It'll heal all your ills."

She rubbed the beard of bubbles that had attached itself to her chin. "I am not a drinking woman."

"You'll drink this."

He came down into the water with her. She thought again what a perfectly beautiful man he was, so big and powerfully built, and yet lean. He had such a fine, economical grace when he moved.

He handed her the whiskey. She sipped, made a face and set it on the wide edge of the tub. He settled in and took a sip himself.

And he watched her.

He was waiting. For her to tell him more. And, against her better judgment, she found that she *wanted* to tell him more. Whatever happened tomorrow, in the bright and too-revealing light of day, tonight she wanted to give him everything. Whatever he wanted of her.

Her body.

Her passion.

Her one sad and awful little secret.

She picked up her glass again, knocked back another sip. She did it too fast, and ended up coughing as the whiskey seared its way down her throat.

"Relax." Cord guided a loose curl behind her ear. "All right?"

She coughed again. "Fine." She'd heard that whiskey was supposed to give a person a little false courage—maybe make a tough situation easier to face. It didn't seem to be helping her all that much. She set the glass down for good.

And she began to talk.

"The summer I turned seventeen, I got a break. A really big break—or at least, that was what it seemed like at the time. I got fostered by a family in Tulsa. A rich family. They didn't even need the money the state pays out for foster kids. They wanted to help out, to do their social duty, you could say. And the woman, my foster mother, she told me when she met me, before she picked me to come and live in her house, that she'd always wanted a daughter. She had two sons, one in his twenties, out on his own by then, and one my age, at home. I went to live with them in May, as soon as school was out. I remember my first sight of the house they lived in...." She stared into the middle distance, remembering.

Cord prompted, "Big?"

Hannah shivered, then sighed. Idly she ran her hand

over the water's surface, flattening bubbles as she went. "Not so big as Stockwell Mansion, but big enough, to an orphan from Oologah. Fifteen rooms, I think it had. A beautiful house, two stories, with columns in front." Hannah leaned her head back against the tub rim and closed her eyes. "My foster mother took me right upstairs to my new bedroom. It had Country French furniture and blue-and-pink striped wallpaper and I thought it was the most beautiful room I'd ever seen. And *then,* while I was standing in the middle of that room, *oohing* and *ahing* my little heart out, my foster brother appeared in the doorway to introduce himself."

Hannah felt the water move. Cord's leg brushed hers. She thought he might say something. But he remained quiet. She kept her eyes closed. It was easier that way.

She said, "He had blue eyes. And thick, dark hair. And when he smiled at me…"

Cord did speak then. "Love at first sight?"

"I thought so at the time. What did I know? I was only seventeen. I'd never even been on a date with a boy. I thought I was in love and I thought he loved me. We started…meeting, in secret, late at night. His room. Or my room. We took crazy chances. And, hard as it is for me to believe now, we never got caught."

"Until you got pregnant."

She sat up in the water and looked at him. She saw no judgment of her in his eyes.

And Hannah was right.

Cord *wasn't* judging her.

He already hated the boy she had given her love to. But he felt only tenderness toward Hannah, toward the sweet, hopeless innocent she must once have been.

"Yes," she said, her pretty face flushed—from the heat

of the water, or perhaps her remembered shame. "By August, I couldn't ignore the signs."

He knew what she would have done. "You told the boy."

She nodded.

"And he...?"

"At first, he said he loved me. That he would marry me. But then..."

"Then what?"

"We told his mother."

"What did she do?"

"She blamed me. Called me a lot of real ugly names, went on about how she'd given me so much, treated me like a daughter—and look how I was paying her back. He was there, the boy, when she said all those horrible things. And he...he didn't defend me. He never spoke up, even once, to admit he'd been part of it, too. She said I seduced him. And he just sat there, looking guilty. Looking like he thought that what she'd said was probably right." Hannah wrapped her soft arms around herself and absently rubbed at the film of bubbles that were melting on her shoulders.

The green eyes were far away, lost in old hurts. "She arranged to have him sent away, to go to school back east. And she sent me away, too. To a halfway house for unwed mothers. I ran away from that place twice. But in the end, I...well, I made peace with my situation, I guess you could say. I was seventeen and I had a baby inside me and I realized that the best thing I could do for my baby would be to stay in the halfway house until she was born."

"And then?"

"And then give her up to a loving mother and father, who would raise her to have everything I lost when I was

nine—the attention, and the laughter, the sharing...
everything you get in a real family.''

''And did you do that?''

She nodded, still absently rubbing her pretty, pale
shoulders. ''I made them let me meet the new parents
before I would sign any of the papers. They were good
people, gentle, kind people. And they were willing to keep
in touch with me, to tell me how Ella Marie was doing—
that was her name, my daughter's. Ella Marie...'' Her
mouth was trembling.

Cord couldn't stand to see that, the way her soft lips
trembled, the stark pain in her eyes. He set his empty glass
on the edge of the tub next to her almost-full one. Then
he gathered her into his arms.

She resisted at first, but then, with a soft exhalation of
breath, she gave in and laid her head against his chest.
They floated there, in the cooling bath, with the bubbles
slowly dissolving around them.

He stroked her damp hair, her nape, her velvety shoulder.

Finally she said, ''Three months after I gave her away,
Ella Marie died.''

Cord held her tighter, placed a kiss in her hair.

''It was a SIDS death.'' He felt her breath against his
chest. ''And I know...it's not logical for me to blame
myself. I know that it wasn't my fault. It was nobody's
fault. But somehow, I've always felt that I could have
made a difference, that I should have kept her. That I was
her mother and if I'd been there, she would have lived...''

Cord had no damn idea what to say to her. He kept
thinking of the boy who had betrayed her: a rich boy,
with dark hair and blue eyes.

And he also thought of Becky. He was learning that it
didn't take long for a baby to claim her place in a parent's

heart. He'd only known he was a father for three weeks. Becky had lived in his rooms for less than two. And yet, if something were to happen to her now, if he were to lose her, she'd leave a huge, ragged hole at the very center of his world.

He whispered, "Hannah. You're right. It *wasn't* your fault…"

She squirmed in his arms, pushing at his chest until he released her enough that she could look into his eyes. "Oh, Cord. I know that. In my mind. It's my heart that just can't seem to get the message."

He stared at her sweet, damp face with the little wisps of soft hair curling at her temples and he wanted to make everything right for her.

He probably shouldn't have offered. But he was who he was. "Do you want them to pay?"

"Pay?" She sat up straighter. "Who?"

"The boy who got you pregnant—though I guess he's a man now. And his mother. That whole family."

She put her hand to her throat. "You mean…*hurt* them?"

"Just give me a name, Hannah. I'll see what I can do."

"But I don't…you're talking about hiring some kind of hit man, or something?"

He let out a laugh. In spite of the tough times she'd been through, in some ways she remained a total naïf. "Murder is a little too…obvious for me. No. I was thinking more on a financial level. I have connections in Tulsa. It would take time, of course, but I can probably arrange for an eventual…how should I put it? A reversal of fortune?"

She gaped. "A reversal of…you are kidding me."

"Hannah, I promise you. I don't kid about money. But it wouldn't be fast, you have to understand. It could take years." He paused. She continued to stare at him. So he added, "Just give me their names."

"No." She scooted away so fast that water and bubbles splashed over the rim of the tub. "I really don't want that."

He fought the urge to yank her back into his arms. "You're certain?"

"Yes. I…it was a long time ago. And I truly don't believe in holding grudges. Besides, I wasn't a total victim in what happened. That woman *had* trusted me. I should have stayed away from her son."

"Are you trying to tell me he didn't pursue you?"

"No. He pursued me. And at first, I tried to resist the attraction. But in the end, I said yes to him. I met him whenever we could sneak away. I did wrong. What *they* did, they have to work out between themselves and God."

"Come on. Don't tell me you wouldn't like to see them pay just a little—for the way that they hurt you, for Ella Marie…"

She sat up so straight, the top curves of her breasts emerged from the water. He could see the tempting nipples, firm and sweet and pink. "No. It was a long time ago and I have honestly forgiven them. And it's certainly not their fault what happened to my little girl. I told you. It's myself I have a hard time forgiving."

"You don't even wonder where the boy is now? If he's happy? If he's married someone else, had children with her?"

An enchanting chestnut curl had drooped too close to her eye. She swiped it away. "Cord. He wasn't the person I thought he was. Why in the world would I care what he's doing now?"

He couldn't help smiling. Clearly she carried no torch

for the idiot who'd betrayed her. It was what he'd wanted to hear.

He shrugged. "All right. Have it your way."

"Well." She gave him one of her huffy looks. "Thank you very much."

"Come back here."

She glared at him.

"Please."

Her expression softened. She glided to him again.

He wrapped his arms around her good and tight. They were silent again, drifting there.

Finally he muttered, "I really am so damn sorry, Hannah…"

She didn't say anything. For a moment, he wondered if she had even heard him.

But then she looked up. Her eyes asked for kisses.

He hadn't had a lot of practice at giving comfort to a woman. But he knew how to please, how to distract, how to make her forget…

He covered her mouth, very lightly, with his own. She sighed, an inviting sort of sound. He deepened the kiss, sliding his tongue between her slightly parted lips. She moaned and shyly allowed her tongue to spar with his.

He let his hand slide down, over her wet, willing curves. When he found her, she gasped. But she didn't say no.

On the contrary, she whispered a sweet, impassioned, "Yes…"

He kissed that yes right off her soft mouth as his hand continued its pleasurable task below.

Chapter Fifteen

In the morning, Cord woke first, just as the sun was rising.

For a few pleasant seconds, he didn't move. He watched Hannah, thinking that she looked so soft and defenseless in sleep. She lay on her side, the covers sliding off her shoulder, her fist tucked into the curve of her chin.

There were tender dark circles beneath her eyes.

He smiled to himself. He had tired her out.

She needed rest. Lots of it.

Because tonight, or whenever the next opportunity presented itself, he intended to tire her out all over again.

Careful not to wake her, he slipped from the bed and tiptoed around the big room, drawing all the curtains. When his gaze fell on the baby monitor, near the hall door, he realized he'd have to take care of Becky right away, before she woke and started squalling and Hannah jumped up to run to her.

He went to a bureau to grab a T-shirt and boxers. In the walk-in closet, he found chinos and a pair of moccasins. Swiftly and silently, he pulled on the clothes. His office was equipped with a full bath. And he kept several changes of clothes there, so he could worry about getting himself more appropriately dressed for the workday once he got downstairs. Scooping up the monitor, he left the bedroom suite and strode down the hall to Becky's room.

When he opened her door, she greeted him, letting out one of those cute little questioning cries of hers. He fed her and changed her and amused her for a while, taking her to the play mat on the floor, which had a mobile with rattles and bright balls dangling from it. She went back to bed with no fussing about an hour and a half after he'd entered her room.

He stood out in the hall for a few minutes, with the monitor turned up all the way, trying to decide how long she would let Hannah sleep if he took the monitor back to the bedroom suite. He could, after all, simply carry it downstairs with him and come back up if Becky needed him.

He decided to chance putting it back—mostly because he knew that when Hannah woke alone in his room, the first thing she'd do would be to look for the monitor. If it wasn't there, she'd have a moment of pure panic, before she rushed to Becky's room to make certain the baby was okay.

He wanted Hannah to get some rest—not have a coronary.

And the more he thought about it, the more it seemed advisable that he leave her some kind of note. He didn't want her to decide he'd deserted her, any more than he wanted her to worry about Becky.

So he detoured to the small desk in the sitting room

opposite the nursery, where he spent several minutes trying to figure out what to write.

Once he'd settled on a few succinct lines, he went back down the hall and ducked inside his door just long enough to put the monitor back where he'd found it and the note under the monitor. He saw, when he went in, that Hannah was still sound asleep. Good. With any luck, it might be an hour or two or even more, before Becky disturbed her.

Tonight, when he kept Hannah up late all over again, he wouldn't feel *quite* so guilty about it.

When Cord got downstairs, it was still early enough that his secretary and the four others he kept on permanent staff in the offices had yet to arrive for work. He entered his private office, rang for Emma to send him coffee and croissants, then went to the closet to see about clothes. Once he'd picked out the day's wardrobe, he proceeded to his private bath, where he showered and shaved.

When he emerged, his breakfast was waiting. He sipped coffee and ate two buttery hot croissants.

At eight-thirty on the nose, his secretary, Audrey Caseman, a model of efficiency with steel-gray hair and a sweet granny's smile, stuck her head in his door and asked him if he wanted to dictate those letters he'd mentioned they needed to get out of the way first thing today.

He started to tell her to bring in her notepad when the phone interrupted him.

It was the house line—his father's line. Damn. The old man must be giving the nurses a hard time again. He signaled Audrey to wait a moment and picked up the phone, already mentally rearranging his schedule to allow for some time in his father's rooms.

''I'm calling a family meeting.'' It was his father's

voice. "Get the rest of them together and come to me now."

What the hell? He hadn't heard the old man sound so good in weeks—sharp and cool. Perfectly coherent.

"You there, Cord? You hear me?"

"Yeah, Dad. I hear you."

Caine made a rumbling sound deep in his throat, a sound reminiscent of thunder before a big storm. "Then get the others and get in here. Now."

"Are you...all right?"

"All right?" his father growled. "You're asking me if I'm all right?"

Cord said nothing. What was there to say?

And Caine answered his own question, anyway. "No, damn you. I am *not* all right. I have cancer. My doctors tell me it has metastasized to the point where I have very few major organs left unaffected. At this precise moment, however, I am in full command of my faculties. I have something to say to you—and to your brothers and sister. I want to say it *now*. Is that clear to you, Cord?"

Cord decided he needed another opinion as to what the hell was going on. "Dad. Is Gunderson there?"

"Where else would he be?"

"Put him on."

A weighted silence, then his father demanded, "What for?"

"Just put him on, Dad. Please."

Caine made another of those thunderous sounds low in his throat—and then he raised the decibel level, as he always did when he suspected he was being crossed. "You don't need to talk to the damn nurse! You need to get the others together and get in here. On the double— while I'm feeling up to telling you what you need to hear."

"Dad. Listen." Cord kept his own tone carefully level. "I'm not doing anything until I talk to Gunderson."

There was another silence, a long one this time. It seemed to Cord that he could actually hear his father's powerful will crackling in thwarted fury over the line.

At last, Caine muttered, "Fine."

The next voice was Gunderson's. "Hello, Mr. Stockwell."

"What's going on there?"

"Er, what exactly do you mean, sir?"

"Is my father as clearheaded as he sounds?"

"Yes, sir," said the nurse. "Your father seems to be feeling just excellent today."

"He's…rational?"

"Yes, sir. Quite rational…at the moment."

Caine must have grabbed the phone back, because it was his voice that Cord heard next. "You've talked to the damn nurse. And you know what I want you to do. Do it now." The line went dead.

Audrey still waited, the soul of patience, in the doorway.

"Sorry," Cord told her. "The dictation will have to wait." She dipped her head in response and retreated, pulling the door silently shut behind her.

Cord got back on the phone and began tracking down his brothers and sister. Luckily, they were all in residence. Kate hadn't left for her office yet, Rafe had got in late the night before—and Jack was down in the kitchen, eating a plate of ham and eggs, which the cook had just prepared for him. They each agreed to meet him in fifteen minutes—in the hall outside Caine's rooms.

At 8:54, Cord, Rafe, Jack and Kate entered their father's suite together.

Caine was sitting up in his hospital bed, gaunt and haggard as ever lately, but so alert it was almost scary. "About damn time," he grumbled. He sent a dismissing glance at each of the two nurses. "Out."

Gunderson and the redhead made themselves scarce.

Caine turned to his children, all four of whom waited, shoulder to shoulder, a few feet from the bed. Those rheumy blue eyes pinned each one in turn—Jack, Kate, Cord and then Rafe.

"I'll be dead damn soon," he muttered flatly.

Kate let out a small cry and took an involuntary step toward the bed.

Caine put up a hand. Kate froze. Caine asked, addressing no one in particular, "What is it with women? Softhearted—and softheaded, too?"

Jack muttered something under his breath. It was something about cold-blooded old men.

Kate turned and touched his hand—a touch Cord knew was intended to remind their older brother to keep his cool. It worked, for the moment anyway. Jack fell silent.

Kate drew back her shoulders. "Sorry, Daddy. I don't know what got into me. For a split second there, I actually felt sorry for you."

Caine grunted. "Well, don't. Just stand there. Listen. That's what I want from you now. It's *all* I want. From any of you." Caine turned those red-rimmed eyes on Jack, daring his oldest son to say more. Jack stared right back. But he did hold his tongue.

Finally Caine shrugged. "There's something that's been…eating away at me, right along with the cancer. It's something I sure as hell never meant to admit to anyone, least of all to the four of you. But now…" He laughed, a dry cackle of sound, utterly devoid of any real humor. "Guess I'm more of a sap than I thought. Or maybe it's just plain old everyday guilt. It won't let an old man rest, not until he's seen to it that what can be done *will* be done to take care of what matters—his family. And that means every last one of them, whatever they did. And wherever the hell they may be now."

He paused, maddeningly, and looked down at his gnarled hands. Cord suspected the worst: that he was drifting back into the strange, twilight world he most often inhabited of late.

But when Caine looked up, his eyes were still reasonably clear. He coughed, a throat-clearing sound. His scrawny chest rattled. He drew himself a wheezing breath and then announced, "It's about your mother."

Cord stood utterly still. His brothers and his sister did the same. The room grew oppressively silent, as they waited there, under the old man's bloodshot, knowing eyes. All the overbearing splendor of the place, the rich brocades and gilded woodwork, seemed to press in on them, thickening the air, making it hard to breathe.

Caine granted them all a ghastly grin. "I see I've got your attention now."

The tension, already on a razor's edge, increased. But no one said a word. They waited to hear more.

And Caine shrugged again. "Your mother never drowned in Stockwell Pond."

Cord heard a gasp—Kate's. His brothers stood utterly silent, as stunned as he was. They had all begun to doubt that there had ever been a drowning. But doubting was one thing. Hearing Caine admit the truth outright in a rational voice was something else altogether.

Caine said it again. "Madelyn didn't drown. That was just a story I made up, so none of you would ever get any ideas that you needed to go off looking for her. She didn't drown. And neither did Brandon. The two of them ran away together, twenty-nine years ago next month."

Chapter Sixteen

The old man had more to say.

They were things he had said before.

But before, he'd been raving. Now, he said those things in a calm, clear voice, his eyes hard and bright. Cord found himself believing that they really might be true.

"Madelyn was pregnant when she left," Caine told them. "Just a few months along. When I learned about the baby, I…well, I raised my hand to her, I admit it. Slapped her around pretty good. I accused her of having Brandon's bastard in her belly. She cried and carried on and denied that the baby was my brother's. But I knew she'd been sneaking around, meeting with him in secret."

Kate had her hand over her mouth. Nonetheless, another gasp escaped her.

Caine pinned her with those cold eyes of his. "Spare me your shocked little noises, Miss Kate. I know you've heard all the old rumors. I believe I even mentioned them myself once or twice. Your mother went behind my back to meet her lover.''

He looked down at his hands again, and then muttered reluctantly, ''In retrospect, I don't even know that I blame her. When a man is dying, he has a lot of time to…reflect on what he did back when. All those years ago, I could have killed her with my bare hands for what I'd decided was her betrayal. But…'' He chortled to himself some more, causing more coughing, which he had a little difficulty getting under control.

Finally he reached for the glass of water on the tray at his elbow. He drank, coughed once more. ''I was hardly a model husband, as we all know. And she, well, she never did get over my sainted brother.''

He sipped again, this time in a thoughtful sort of way. ''She was always transparent as a clear sheet of glass. Wore her feelings on those pretty, flowing sleeves of hers. Never did get a handle on how to hide what she felt.'' He set the glass down. ''You'd think she *would* have learned, wouldn't you, living with me?''

Jack spoke up then. ''I'd like a few specifics. What do you mean, she never really got over Uncle Brandon?''

Caine grunted. He looked at his least favorite son with the strangest expression—a crafty look, and a wary one, too. ''She loved him. Before she married me. She would have married *him* instead of me. But I fixed that.''

''You fixed that *how?*''

Caine waved his hand, dismissing the question. ''We don't need to go into all that now.''

''You're wrong.'' Jack's voice was hard as stone. ''We do.''

Caine's grizzled brows drew together. He made that thunderous sound in his throat. ''I said no.''

Jack refused to back down. ''And I said yes.''

The two glared at each other, Jack's face revealing nothing, Caine's contorting with rage. In the old days, Caine would have acted on his wrath. Jack would have taken a number of blows from Caine's powerful arm.

But Caine's body was wasted now, his arms little more than brittle sticks. Now, instead of striking out, he shouted, "You don't run things around here, mister! And you never will. I'll tell you what I want to tell you, and if you don't back off, I won't you tell a damn thing." The shouting brought on a coughing fit.

Jack waited for the cough to subside a little before he said, "You heartless piece of—"

Cord was the one who intervened that time. "Jack." He put a steadying hand on his older brother's rock-hard shoulder. "Don't. He'll never tell us what he started to say."

In response to that, Caine threw back his head and crowed at the crystal-and-gold chandelier overhead. "Cord's got it right." He had to pause, to cough some more. "Better listen to him. And listen to *me*. You get what *I* want to tell you, Jack, and that's all you get."

Jack stared at his father, a muscle working fiercely in his jaw. Kate, on his other side, put her hand on his arm. "Please, Jack..."

Jack swung his furious gaze on Kate. He looked at her for a long time. At last, he nodded. "All right. Let him talk." He sent Cord a rueful glance. "You can let go, too. I won't kill him. Not today, anyway."

Caine was grinning again. On him, the expression reeked of pure malice. "I've missed the family drama, I must say I have."

"Get on with it," Cord commanded.

Miraculously, Caine did.

"All right. Where was I? Ah. I remember now. They

ran off together, your mother and my holier-than-thou, back-stabbing twin brother, on Independence Day—and no, the irony does not escape me—twenty-nine years ago. You—at least you three—'' he was looking at his sons ''—wouldn't shut up about that damn woman. Each of you, over and over, 'Where is she?' 'I want my mother.' 'Where is my mother?' Kate, blessedly, didn't ask much at all, since she only knew a few words at the time. I got sick of the questions, so I made up the story of how sweet Madelyn and my brother had drowned in a rowboat out on the pond. I found it very...satisfying, to tell you. And to tell you again. And again. And again.

''I fired all the servants, hired a whole new staff, so I could be certain you'd never hear the truth from a maid or a gardener. And I made sure that my business associates, the ones who came to the house regularly, found it to be in their best interests to go along with the lie.

''It's surprising how impressionable a young mind can be. At first, you wouldn't believe me—especially you, Jackie boy. But I had the years on my side. I had...all the power on my side. By the time you all reached your teens, you were thoroughly indoctrinated. You never questioned the logic of any of it. You believed what I had told you: that your mother was long dead, that she had died in a boating accident—and that her body was never found.''

Jack asked the question that was screaming through all of their minds. ''Where is she now?''

Caine blinked. And shook his head. Then he closed his eyes.

Cord swore. ''He's fading.''

''Dad?'' prompted Rafe. ''Dad? Where is Madelyn now?''

Caine opened his eyes. ''Not finished. What? Oh. The thing is, the more I think about it, the more certain I am that the baby was mine. She had a...damn disgusting high moral sense, that mother of yours. She might have sneaked around behind my back, meeting with my brother, crying on his shoulder because I made her life such a misery, but I don't think she was lifting her pretty skirts for him—not then, anyway.

"And though I didn't come to her bed that often by then, I came enough. So it was mine, that baby. *My* baby. And no matter what the hell you say about me, I'm a Stockwell, and I take care of my own.

"I've sent money for that baby—and for Madelyn, too—every month of every year since she ran off. I've tried, damn it, to do the right thing. It's not my fault that all the checks just came back."

"Where is she?" Jack said again.

But Caine was groaning, now, tossing his head from side to side. "That's all. That's all. Now you know. She didn't drown..."

"Answer me," demanded Jack.

"Out. Out. All of you. 'Cept for Cord. I don't want you others here. No more...get out..."

Jack stepped toward the bed, sheer fury burning in his eyes again. But Kate grabbed him back. "Please, Jack. Look at him. He's not going to say anymore."

"Out!" The lax tendons in Caine's raddled neck leaped into taut relief as he threw back his gaunt head and bellowed. "All of you...out!" He coughed and beat his fist on the edge of the bed. "Cord. Here. Here to me..."

"Give me a few minutes with him," Cord said, stepping forward with a weary wave. "Then send the nurses in."

Rafe said, "Cord, you don't have to—"

"It's all right. I'll take it from here."

Caine's wasted arm shot out. He grabbed Cord by the shoulder. "Cord. Here. Listen. Have to tell you…"

Cord peeled the bony fingers off his shirt. "Go. Please," he said to the others.

They turned, reluctantly, and filed out.

"*My* son. *My* flesh…" the old man muttered. "Just like me. Remember that. Like me. We understand each other. Me and you. We're the same…" He chortled to himself, stopped just short of a coughing fit. "No. Not quite the same. You're smarter than your old man, aren't you? Never let yourself get hooked up with one woman. You know that only leads to disaster, for a man like you, a man like me…"

Cord hated the way he felt right then: torn right down the middle—between revulsion and pity.

Caine raved some more. "You do what you have to do. Find Madelyn. And the child. But watch out for those others, now. Don't let them convince you to give away what's ours. I didn't let Brandon do it. You hold firm, too. Hold firm, hold on. The land and the oil underneath it…Stockwell land now. Stockwell oil…"

Cord sat on the edge of the bed and let his father babble away. Soon enough, Gunderson appeared. He got the syringe ready. Cord left as soon as the narcotic took effect.

The others were waiting for him out in the hall.

"Well?" Rafe asked, as soon as Cord pulled the door closed behind him.

"He's sleeping now, for a while, at least."

"Did he say anything else?" Jack asked. "About Madelyn? Or Brandon? Or any of it?"

"He said…to do what I had to do to find Madelyn and the 'baby,' and he also made reference to the land deal, I think. He told me to 'hold on.' Not to let 'those others' talk me into giving up what's ours."

''Those others,'' Kate said wryly. ''That would be Jack, Rafe and me, I suppose?''

Cord shrugged. '''Fraid so. Our father has the impression that I'm every bit as unscrupulous as he is.''

Jack made a low, disgusted sound.

''We're glad he's wrong,'' said Kate fondly. It felt good, to hear her confident reassurance that he was not the same man their father was.

Rafe swore. ''All these years. We *believed* what he told us...at least *I* always did.''

Kate nodded. ''I did, too. I never doubted. Did you, Jack?''

''I wondered. But eventually, I got to the point where I decided it was only wishful thinking.''

''We were children,'' Cord reminded them. ''And he said it himself. He had all the power.''

Rafe was shaking his head. ''Still, we should have—''

''No,'' Cord said. ''There's no point in beating ourselves up for what we might have done. Let's concentrate on doing whatever we can to straighten things out *now*.'' He ran his fingers back through his hair, trying to remember if there was anything else of importance he needed to tell them.

It came to him. ''Oh—and another thing. Just now, he also mentioned Uncle Brandon again. When he told me I wasn't to let you talk me into giving away what was ours, he said that he hadn't let Brandon do it. He's mentioned that more than once now, that Brandon knew about the land deal. He said I was to 'hold firm' and 'hold on' to the land, and the oil underneath it—as he, Caine, had done. It was pretty disjointed, but he also babbled out something about how it was Stockwell land now and Stockwell oil, too.''

Rafe shook his head. ''Damn. What a mess.''

"Yeah," Cord agreed. "But we do have a little more than we had before. We have it straight from his own mouth—in reasonably lucid form for once—that Madelyn and our uncle didn't die all those years ago. It appears that Madelyn *was* pregnant. Which means we may have another brother or sister somewhere in the world."

Jack was nodding. "And he mentioned he's been sending them money. Every month, he said, for the last twenty-nine years. We just might be able to trace a money trail."

The four traded glances.

"I can check his personal accounts," Cord said. "But I imagine it's not going to be quite that simple. He would have made a real effort to hide the expenditures, so no one else would stumble on them by accident."

"Okay," Kate said. "So if the money hasn't been coming out of his personal checkbook, then where do we look for it?"

Cord had a few ideas. "I've been working to get all the company records put on computer. Whatever's in the system now, I would know about—or at least, I'd have easy access to. But until six months ago, Dad still ran a few things himself. And he never did bother to learn how to make a spreadsheet. So there are…loose ends. I keep meaning to get it all cleaned up and into the system, but I haven't gone through everything he was up to as of yet."

Jack asked, "Where is *everything he was up to?*"

"When I took over his office, I had all of his stuff stored in the basement. His office furniture is down there, along with several boxes full of papers and correspondence, as well as two four-drawer file cabinets."

Jack said, "Let's not get ahead of ourselves. Even though I doubt we'll find anything there, we need to eliminate the obvious first."

Kate nodded. "His checkbook."

"I'll bet it's in that little desk in his sitting room," Cord suggested. "Give me a minute." He turned and reentered his father's suite.

Gunderson glanced over with a questioning expression as Cord pushed the door shut behind him. Cord shook his head and Gunderson looked away. The wasted figure on the hospital bed lay still, eyes shut, snoring steadily.

Cord turned to the gilded desk. He found the large, professional-style leather-bound checkbook in the first drawer he opened. Quickly he scanned the pages of the register, which went back a year and four months. He found no suspicious-looking monthly entries. He put it away and then spent a few minutes going through the drawers and other various nooks and crannies the desk contained. He came up with nothing that might aid in the search for Madelyn and Brandon.

He did, however, find a key ring with about ten keys on it of varying sizes, keys that could go to just about anything. The keys jangled as he dropped the ring into his pocket, thinking that one of them might let him in to the file cabinets in the basement. He didn't recall whether they were locked or not.

A few minutes after he'd left them, he rejoined his brothers and sisters in the hall.

"Well?" asked Jack.

"Nothing—at least not in there. The statements for that account for the past five or six years, anyway, are probably in the basement with just about everything else. So I'll review them, too, when I find them." He dragged in a fortifying breath. "There's a mountain of paper down there. I think I'd better get started."

Jack said, "You think we're going to let you tackle this alone?"

Cord looked from one determined face to the next. "It could take a while. I'm not kidding. There's a lot of paper downstairs."

Jack didn't hesitate. "I'm all yours, for as long as you need me."

Rafe spoke up. "I'm free today."

Kate was willing, too. "I can make a few calls, rearrange my schedule so I can take off today."

"Then let's get started," Jack advised. "Let's find out how and where Caine sent that money."

Kate sighed. "If he really did send any money. If he was telling the truth today. If any of this is any more than the pitiful delusions of a dying man."

"We know there's something to it, Kate," Rafe reminded her. "We know there's no record of anyone drowning in Stockwell Pond twenty-nine years ago. There's no grave, either. Did you ever think of that? If Caine really believed they had died, don't you think he would have put up something, some memorial to the fact that they were no longer on this earth?"

"Rafe's right," said Jack. "What the old man told us today makes an evil kind of sense. Madelyn and Brandon are alive—or at least, they *were* alive when they ran off twenty-nine years ago."

The basement of Stockwell Mansion was a maze of dark chambers. At its heart lay a large wine cellar and a professional-style gymnasium, with exercise machines, mirrored walls and a free-weight area. Branching out from there were a number of small finished rooms where servants often lived. Beyond the finished rooms, corridor after poorly lighted corridor led to storage areas for everything from kitchen goods to discarded furniture to old toys that generations of Stockwell children had long ago outgrown.

Cord took them to the room where he'd stored the contents of their father's office. He flipped the wall switch and the bare two-hundred-watt bulb in the ceiling popped on, blinding them all momentarily with the glare.

"Lovely," said Kate, wrinkling her fine nose as she surveyed the dusty stacks of boxes, the jumble of furniture and file cabinets. "Where do we start?"

Cord quickly improvised a plan. Jack and Kate would each take a file cabinet. Cord and Rafe would split the piles of boxes between them.

Kate asked if they'd give her a few minutes before she began. "I've got to make those calls I mentioned, to reschedule my appointments for another day."

Cord remembered poor Audrey, still waiting to take that dictation.

And Hannah.

Just thinking about her gave him pleasure. Was she still asleep? He glanced at his watch. Not ten yet. No way to tell from down here in the basement if she was up and about, or still dreaming in his bed.

"Now that you mention it," he said. "I should probably go check in at the office, tell Audrey where to look if some emergency comes up—and make a call or two myself."

"Good enough." Rafe swung a file box onto their father's huge, heavily carved mahogany desk and took off the lid. "Jack and I will get started."

Jack was already pulling open the top drawer of a file cabinet. "You two get your commitments handled and get back down here ASAP."

Cord rode the service elevator up with Kate. He considered going all the way to the second floor with her. He could look in on Becky—and Hannah.

But no.

Right now, business had to come before pleasure. He got off on the first floor. He went to his office, called Audrey in and told her regretfully that they'd have to put off that dictation till tomorrow, after all.

"Good enough," Audrey said. "Oh, that reporter from *Inside Scoop* called again. Pushy as ever. He still wants an interview."

Cord had been dodging that particular reporter for days. He suspected the man might have heard about Becky. But he wasn't going to find out. In his experience, it never helped to talk to the tabloids. They only twisted what they heard. Better to let them do their worst—and then sue, if it came down to that.

"Tell him, again, that I have nothing to say."

Audrey gave him her sweetest, most grandmotherly grin. "Will do."

He let Audrey go and made the necessary calls. By ten-thirty, he was ready to join the others downstairs.

He felt certain, by then, that Hannah would be awake. No way Becky would nap much past ten.

He wanted to run upstairs, just for a minute or two. To share a few tender, teasing words, steal a kiss—or maybe five.

He was grinning like a fool.

He didn't really understand what was happening to him when it came to Hannah. Never had he felt quite this captivated by a woman. Anticipatory of the next encounter, yes. But not so…inexorably drawn. Considering the stacks of boxes that waited in the basement and all the work he *wouldn't* get done today, a woman should be the last thing on his mind.

Not so. Hannah Miller kept insinuating herself front and center in his thoughts.

Better *not* to call her. He'd only be all the more tempted to drop everything and run upstairs to her side.

Tonight, he thought.

After he'd worked all day beside his brothers and sister trying to track down a lead or two on where his mother and his uncle and possibly his lost brother or sister were now…

Tonight, he could claim his reward.

Instead of buzzing the nanny's room, he got Emma on the line. "I want twelve dozen pink roses delivered to Hannah's room within the hour. When you talk to the florist, tell them I don't want those damn buds that never bloom. I want the best, and I want them to *smell* like roses."

"And the card?"

"It should read, 'I can't make it for our walk today—but I *will* make it up to you.' Have them underline 'will.'"

"Signed with your name?"

"No. She'll know who sent them."

"Anything else?"

"That'll be it for now. Thank you, Emma."

He called Tiffany's next and ordered a pin he'd always admired. It was shaped like a starfish, set with cabochon sapphires, a single ruby at its heart. The salesman assured him that the pin would arrive at the mansion within twenty-four hours. Cord would present it to Hannah tomorrow night, their third night together—the third of a long, enchanting string of magical nights to come.

Hannah really was different than any other woman he'd ever known. She made him laugh and she made him think. And in bed, she was a miracle. Innocent. And passionate.

Shy and yet so willing. It would be a long time before he became tired of her.

As he hung up the phone and went to join the others downstairs, he couldn't help wondering just what she might be doing now....

Chapter Seventeen

Hannah pushed her tangled hair away from her face, gathered the robe she'd just pulled on closer around her and stared down at the words that Cord had written.

You're so sweet when you're sleeping. I didn't want to wake you. I'm hoping my daughter will let you sleep just a little while longer.

From the monitor, Becky wailed.

Hannah blinked the sleep from her eyes. Lordy. The fancy marble clock on the dresser said it was quarter of eleven. How could she possibly have slept that long?

Oh, come on, she thought a moment later, what's so surprising? You went to sleep *when?*

It had been very late—after three.

Hannah felt her face flushing—for heaven's sake, her whole body was turning red, every square inch of skin just burning up—with embarrassment at the memory of what she'd been doing when she *should* have been sleeping.

Not to mention what she'd been saying. Sweet Lord, she'd told him *everything*. She must have been out of her mind.

From the monitor, she heard Becky suck in a long breath—and then wail all the louder.

"I'm coming, darlin'," Hannah whispered soothingly, as if the little one could actually hear her. "I'm on my way…"

She grabbed the monitor and made for the door to the hall.

By the time Hannah reached her side, Becky's little face was purple as a pickled beet with baby frustration. Hannah scooped her up and carried her over to change her diaper. Once that was accomplished, she got the bottle warmed fast and gave Becky her late-morning snack. She was just raising her to burp her when the phone on the wall of the playroom buzzed—the house line. Hannah rose from the rocker, Becky on her shoulder, and hurried into the adjacent room.

"Ms. Miller?" It was the calm, cool voice of the housekeeper.

Hannah's face went burning red all over again—as if Stockwell Mansion's head housekeeper knew or even cared what Hannah and her employer had been doing all night long. "Um. Yes, Mrs. Hightower? What can I do for you?"

"A Miss Ada Sessions is here to see you."

Ada Sessions? Hannah's mind went blank.

Then she remembered.

The first nanny candidate of the day. Due at eleven. How could she have let herself forget?

"Ms. Miller? Are you still there?"

"Yes, Mrs. Hightower. Could you please ask her to wait a few minutes?"

"Of course. Call when you'd like her sent up."

The line went dead and Becky burped. Hannah hung up the phone, grabbed Becky's baby seat from the corner and fled to the small bathroom off the nanny's room. There, she strapped Becky into the seat and left her, fussing a little, on the floor, as she took the world's swiftest shower. Then she flew around her bedroom, grabbing underwear, a shirt, a skirt and a pair of ballet-style flats.

Once she had her clothes on, she got a scrunchy from the bathroom drawer and quickly smoothed her hair into a ponytail. Finally, murmuring reassurances to the slightly disgruntled baby the whole time, she slapped on a bit of blusher, mascara and some lip-gloss.

There. She looked a little frazzled, a little thrown-together—but then, frazzled and thrown-together was exactly how she felt.

She called Emma back and asked her to send the applicant on up.

Ada Sessions was twenty years old. She had worked as a nanny for six months, for a family that had recently moved out of state.

Ada was very impressed with the house and the grounds. "I am, like, blown away. What a place. Like a palace kinda, huh?"

Hannah thought, No way. Too young, too wide-eyed, and much too flighty. Becky requires someone mature...

But then she caught herself.

No one, in the end, would ever be good enough. She couldn't just go on rejecting every applicant out of hand the minute they opened their mouths. No. After what had happened last night, she simply had to take action.

What *was* she now, for heaven's sake? Cord Stockwell's mistress? The idea appalled her. She simply was not the mistress type. Then again, maybe "mistress" didn't apply to her, anyway. The word mistress, after all, implied an ongoing intimate relationship.

So far, the intimacy had only lasted one night.

So was that it, what she and Cord had shared? Did she fall into the category of a one-night stand?

Oh, good grief. What did it matter what she called herself—except for extremely foolish, which she definitely was.

It wasn't going to happen again. *That* was what mattered.

Becky might be only a baby, but Hannah did want the best for her. And the best for her did *not* include having her nanny and her daddy carrying on down the hall.

Hannah knew that if she stayed it *would* happen again. And again and again, until the inevitable occurred and Cord grew tired of her.

So she would fix things. She would choose her replacement, which she should have done long before now.

She had five candidates to meet with today. One of them *would* be the one.

She asked Ada about her schooling, about the children the girl had taken care of before. The interview was going pretty well—until three men appeared in the hall, each carrying a huge crystal vase full of pink roses.

"Delivery for Miss Hannah Miller," announced the oldest of the men, a jolly fellow with a full beard and a Santa-size stomach. He actually winked at her.

Hannah was forced to excuse herself. She asked Ada, whose eyes had gone so wide that they threatened to swallow her rather narrow face, to watch Becky for just a few moments.

"Oh, wow, sure. No problem, Ms. Miller. Sheesh,

that's a lot of roses. From your boyfriend? He must be so romantic. And a big spender, too. Roses are not cheap."

Hannah pretended she hadn't heard the question about the boyfriend, promised again to return in a minute, and went to lead the men to her room. They set the vases down—two on the bureau and one beside the TV.

"We'll be right back," promised the one who looked like Santa.

"Right back?" Hannah repeated rather stupidly.

The Santa delivery man chuckled. "Sure enough. We've got twelve dozen total. This is only the first six."

Hannah said nothing. What could she say? She didn't think she'd ever seen twelve dozen roses in one room in her lifetime.

She opened the card while they were gone and felt that dangerous warmth in her midsection when she read how Cord intended to "make it up" to her for missing their daily walk.

The roses were so beautiful. They actually seemed to glow...

And three more vases of them, two dozen each, appeared a few minutes later.

The bearded fellow winked a second time. "Whoever he is, I'd say he's smitten."

Smitten? Hannah thought. Cord Stockwell, *smitten?* My goodness, could that be true?

No. She had to be realistic about this. Cord enjoyed women. And he had plenty of money to lavish on them. Such extravagant gestures were probably part of his usual routine, whenever he started in with someone new.

The three men filed out.

Hannah lingered in her bedroom, which had become a pink bower. The scent of the roses swam in the air. She was ashamed to admit it to herself, but she could have sat on the edge of her bed, sniffing and staring, for hours.

However, Ada Sessions was waiting for her to finish their interview. Hannah resolutely turned for the door to the playroom. Ada might not be the right one. But the right one *would* come today. The right one *had* to come.

And all the beautiful roses?

They had to go.

At three in the afternoon, in the tenth box he went through, Cord found statements from an account he hadn't known existed. One check a month, for a significant sum, had been written on that account. The statements went back seven years. The checks were made out to Clyde Carlyle, Attorney at Law.

They all knew the name, of course. For decades, Carlyle had handled all the personal legal matters of the Stockwell family. Rafe and Carlyle's daughter, Caroline, who ran the Carlyle law offices now, had even dated for a while.

"Check under 'Carlyle' in the files," Cord told Jack, who had the cabinet with the *C*'s in it.

"I've been through all the *C*'s," Jack grumbled.

"Well, look up 'Carlyle' again."

Jack pulled out the file in question and flipped it open. They all gathered around as he ran through the pages of correspondence and legal documents inside. There was nothing in it that had anything to do with the mysterious account.

"So we'll have to pay him a visit," Jack said, shutting the file and sticking it back into the cabinet.

Rafe was shaking his head. "Clyde Carlyle's in a rest home. Maybe you didn't hear. It's Alzheimer's and it's pretty far advanced."

Jack shrugged. "Talk to the daughter, then."

Rafe didn't look terribly excited at the prospect.

Cord could read his twin reasonably well—well enough to be certain there was something going on here. Cord hadn't seen Caroline in months, now that he thought about it, though for a while there, she and Rafe had been tight. He wondered what had gone down between his twin and Clyde Carlyle's daughter. Since Rafe never talked about his love life, Cord doubted he'd ever be too likely to find out.

And now was certainly not the time to ask. They had plenty of files and boxes to get through yet. He suggested, "Let's finish going through the rest of this stuff. Maybe we'll find something that will tell us more."

They returned to the dull work of reading dusty, yellowed papers that no one had so much as glanced at in years.

At five, Kate ran upstairs to ask Emma to send down some sandwiches. The trays of food arrived and they cleared a space on the desk for the maids to set it all down. Then they took turns at the sink in the dank half bath midway down the corridor, each making an attempt to rinse off the dust.

Finally they pulled a few chairs out of the jumble of furniture and made themselves comfortable. The food tasted wonderful to Cord. He hadn't eaten since those two croissants that morning. He was on his second sandwich, his mind, as it had been doing all day, wandering off to thoughts of Hannah, when Kate, who had perched on the corner of their father's massive old desk, snagged her right trouser leg on a section of carved woodwork.

She let out a moan. "I love these pants. And now they'll have a pull."

Rafe lifted an eyebrow. "Should have changed into something more practical."

Kate faked a haughty tone. "Practical? I don't do practical. You know very well that fashion is my life."

"Hold still." Jack got up and set his plate on his chair. "I'll see if I can free it without making it worse." Kneeling, he gently unsnagged the caught thread.

"You're my hero, Jack." Kate made a big show of putting her hand to her heart.

Jack wasn't listening. "What's this?"

Cord sat forward—and saw another drawer built into the outer edge of the desk, a drawer cleverly disguised by the ornate carving of the woodwork.

"Look at this," said Jack, pushing aside a tiny flap. "A keyhole."

Kate slid out of his way and onto her feet. "Well, what do you know?"

Cord felt in his pocket for the key ring he'd found in his father's desk upstairs. "Try one of these." He tossed the keys to Jack.

The third one Jack tried was a match. He turned the tiny key and pulled open the drawer.

There were three yellowed envelopes inside, all addressed to Caine Stockwell. Jack carefully removed the contents of each envelope and smoothed the pages.

"What do they say?" Kate prompted eagerly.

"Just a minute…" Jack scanned each letter. It didn't take him long.

"Well?" demanded Rafe.

Jack handed Rafe the short stack of brittle paper. "See for yourself."

Rafe studied the first letter. "They're from a Mr. Gabriel Johnson…"

Jack nodded. "Right. Gabriel Johnson of Rose Hill,

Texas. He claims to be a direct descendant of Miles Johnson, who lost so much so mysteriously back around 1900. He insists, in each of the letters—and in each one he seems angrier than in the one before—that the Johnsons were robbed by the first Caine Stockwell. He demands some form of restitution, and he swears that he can show proof of his claim.''

"What kind of proof?" Cord stood and set his empty plate on one of the trays in the center of the desk.

Rafe was still reading. "He's pretty vague about that."

Cord looked over his twin's shoulder. "That's all? A claim, and a promise that there *is* proof."

Rafe finished scanning the final page. "That's right. There's nothing solid here, other than the name and the address."

Kate took the letters from him, refolded them, and put them back into their envelopes. "Okay, we've got these letters. And the mysterious checks made out to Clyde Carlyle. Let's plow through the rest of this stuff and see if we can come up with anything else."

By seven, they had searched every file and scoured every box. And they still had nothing more to go on than the three letters from Gabriel Johnson and the mysterious bank account with its large monthly payments to Clyde Carlyle.

"Looks like somebody needs to visit Caroline Carlyle," Jack said. "And it will probably also be necessary to see if we can track down this Gabriel Johnson—or his children, if he's no longer around."

"*I'll* talk to Caroline," Rafe announced, sounding grim. "But it'll have to wait a few days. I have to go out of state again first thing tomorrow. But I'll get in touch with her as soon as I get back."

"Fine," said Jack. "And eventually, I'll go looking for Gabriel Johnson. But I'd like to spend a few days down here in the basement first."

"How exciting," said Kate, her tone making it clear that she really thought it was anything but.

Jack shrugged. "I'll go through all of this stuff again. You never know what I might find on a closer look." He held up the key ring Cord had tossed him before. "Maybe I'll find some more places to use these—and Cord, in the meantime…"

"I know, I know. Whatever information I can get out of the old man…"

"Anything could help."

"I'll do what I can."

Cord swore he could smell the scent of roses drifting in the air when he reached his rooms about ten minutes later.

Had she liked the roses he'd sent? He wished he'd been there to see her face when they arrived.

But he'd done his duty first.

And now, he could seek his reward.

As soon as he cleaned up a little. He felt grimy—and he was—from the dusty work downstairs. His shirt was wrinkled and streaked with dirt, same for his slacks. He'd taken off his tie hours ago, left it somewhere downstairs draped over a chair or a box. Hell if he remembered exactly where.

He needed a shower before he went to Hannah, before he held his daughter in his arms. The doors to the nursery suite were all shut, which was fine with him. Hannah wouldn't see him go by and wonder why he hadn't sought her out immediately.

In his bedroom, all was in order. The maids had done

their work, erasing every sign of the night before—except for the white nightgown. It was folded neatly, laid on the bed.

She had left it behind. Cord could see it just as it must have happened...

Becky had wakened her with a cry. She'd pulled on that green robe, skipping the nightgown, in a hurry to get to the baby.

He paused at the side of the bed, ran his hand over the snowy cotton. Soft. There was no one to see, so he indulged himself. He picked up the folded gown and pressed his face into it.

Flowers. Baby lotion. Incredible sweetness.

Hannah.

With great care, he set the gown back on the bed. He would return it to her tonight, ask her to wear it again, and soon, so that he could have the pleasure of taking it off of her—and he was wasting precious time. Time that could be spent with Hannah.

He headed for the bathroom, peeling his filthy clothes off as he went. It took him ten minutes, total, to shower and to dress again, this time in chinos and a polo shirt. He left his room and went down the hall to the nursery.

He tried Becky's bedroom first, pushing the door open quietly. She lay in her crib, sound asleep as he'd suspected she might be. He stood over her for a moment, marveling again at how beautiful, how perfect, how incredible she was. Then he went out through the playroom, shutting the door soundlessly behind him.

He hesitated before he knocked at Hannah's door.

Damn. All of a sudden, he was as nervous as a kid with a first crush. What if she—?

What if she *what?*

Didn't answer? Wasn't there?

Of course she was there. Where else would she be, with his daughter asleep in her bed a room away? He was glad he'd seen to it that she got a little extra sleep, because it would be a long night. He wanted to tell her everything that had happened that day, from the bizarrely lucid things his father had said to the hours in the basement, which had resulted in two more clues to the various family mysteries. He wanted to hear what she thought of all of it, to get her take on it.

And after that, he wanted to make love—slowly, deliciously, for a very long time. He raised his hand and knocked. A few seconds later, she pulled back the door. His heart stopped—and then resumed beating just a little too fast.

Something was wrong.

She looked...distant. Careful. Less than thrilled at the sight of him.

His gaze tracked down her body, the body he had so thoroughly enjoyed the night before, now modestly covered with a cotton shirt, a simple A-line skirt.

And shoes.

Something wasn't right.

Hannah never wore shoes in the privacy of her own room.

And where were the roses he'd sent? He scanned the space behind her. Not a damn perfect pink flower in sight. What the hell? Hadn't they been delivered?

Someone was in big trouble. Someone was going to be very sorry about this particular mix-up.

She forced a smile. He hated that, watching her mouth stretch in such a stiff, unwilling fashion. "I...the roses were beautiful. But I couldn't accept them."

He tried to absorb what she was telling him. The roses *had* been delivered, but she had *refused* them?

She continued, "I had Mrs. Hightower take them downstairs to the library, the parlor..." she hesitated, gave a tiny, embarrassed shrug. "Wherever there was room for them. You know what I mean."

"You didn't want the roses?" he heard himself say, his voice slow, thick, like an idiot. He felt like an idiot. A dolt. A dunce. A stammering fool. He wasn't accustomed to feeling like a fool. And he didn't like it at all.

She put her hand to the base of her throat, the way she did when she was anxious. "Please. I didn't say I didn't *want* them."

"You refused them. It's the same damn thing."

"I just...Cord, I really don't think—"

"You don't think what?"

"Well, I..."

"You what?"

"It doesn't matter. Whatever. Thank you for the roses, but, well, I couldn't keep them."

"You *couldn't?*"

"Oh, please. I couldn't. I didn't. It's all the same. Just let it be, will you?"

"Let it be," he repeated, still in village idiot mode.

"Right. Let it be. The fact is, I didn't accept the roses."

"Got that." He wanted to reach out and shake her. "Loud and clear."

"And I...I have some news for you."

He almost echoed her again, almost muttered, "You have news..." But somehow, he managed to keep his mouth shut.

"I've finally found the right nanny," she said. "Oh, Cord, she's really just perfect, warm and loving, extremely capable, with a great sense of humor and an impressive list of references. Her name is Bridget—Bridget O'Hara—and she's willing to start work on Monday."

Chapter Eighteen

Fool, Cord thought. Idiot. Dunce.

He'd spent his whole day anticipating, awaiting the moment he would see her again.

And what had she been doing?

Interviews. One after the other, until she came up with someone who would do as her replacement.

What had she told him last night? That for two weeks, she'd been turning away perfectly good candidates for the job, because deep in her heart she didn't want to leave Becky—or him.

Well, she was certainly singing a different tune now.

She was just chockful of news. "I did want you to meet Bridget first, before I made the final decision. I kept her here for over an hour, thinking that you might come upstairs. I even called your office, but your secretary said you weren't there right then." She added on a rising inflection, "I left a message." As if that proved some-thing—what, he hadn't a clue.

He thought of all he'd been waiting all day to tell her. He didn't want to tell her a damn thing now. "Something came up," he said. "I left the office early and never got back there. I didn't get your message."

"Oh." She gave him a sheepish little smile. "I see. Well. Bridget will be here at eight Monday morning, ready to go. I just know you're going to love her."

"I'm sure I will." He spoke without inflection. "It looks like you've got everything all worked out."

"Yes, well...I did tell you, didn't I, that I needed to be back at work on Monday? Well, I've called my office and told them I can make it in by noon. And I do have to get myself home one of these days," she said. "I've got a lot of houseplants. My neighbor's supposed to be watering them, but, well, they always suffer if I'm gone too long." She coughed—an embarrassed sort of sound. As if it had just occurred to her that he probably didn't give a good damn about her houseplants.

She kept on. "I'll spend a few hours with Bridget, get-ting her moved in, showing her where everything is, and then, that'll be it. I'll have all my things packed and I'll just...take off."

For the first time in his life, he found himself thinking that his coldhearted SOB of a father was right. No woman should ever be allowed to get too close. Somehow—and he still wasn't quite sure how it had happened—he'd let himself start to feel close to this woman.

And look at him now, standing here, feeling sucker-punched, as she explained oh-so-cheerfully how she was walking out of his life. "Monday, then," he heard himself say. "You'll be out of here before noon."

Her fake smile trembled, the perky facade cracking just a little. "Oh, Cord. You know it really is best that I go."

Did he know that? Hell. He didn't know much of anything right at that moment. But he'd be damned if he'd make a bigger fool of himself than he already had. He wouldn't be reduced to begging her to stay.

He shrugged. "You're probably right. And I trust your judgment when it comes to the new nanny. I'm sure that this Bridget O'Hara will work out just fine."

He turned and left her standing there.

When he got out into the hallway, he didn't know what to do with himself. He was facing the central upper hall and the main staircase there, so he blindly kept moving that way. He went down, to the main hall.

Damned if there wasn't a vase of pink roses on the marble-topped table near the front door. He wandered into the parlor. There were two vases of roses in there. And there were three, spaced at even intervals, on the long table in the dining room. He picked up the dining-room extension and buzzed Emma.

When she answered, he told her he wanted her to get rid of the roses. All of them. And he wanted her to do it now.

Emma was a rock, as always. She didn't ask any questions, she didn't give him any arguments. She simply replied, "Of course, Mr. Stockwell. I'll take care of it immediately."

The weekend was a nightmare.

Every time he visited the nursery, Hannah made herself scarce. It irritated the hell out of him, to watch those green eyes widen with distress at the sight of him.

Obviously just being in his presence was painful for her.

Well, it wasn't the best time he'd ever had, either, to see her, and to know that all she wanted was to get away from him. If he'd only had himself to consider, he would have avoided the nursery altogether.

But he couldn't do that. He was a father. A father couldn't just stop seeing his child because the sight of her nanny made him utterly miserable. He forced himself to spend the same amount of time with Becky as he'd spent with her before he had become Ms. Hannah Miller's least favorite person.

On Saturday morning, the starfish pin arrived from Tiffany's. Emma signed for it and then had it sent up to his rooms. He tossed it into a drawer, thinking that eventually he'd get around to returning it.

And he still had the white nightgown. He'd tucked it away on a shelf in the closet. Saturday went by, and she never asked for it. He decided that if she wanted it, she could damn well ask him for it—which she would probably never do, since she practically ran from the nursery every time he entered it.

Saturday about six, Kate called from downstairs. She was with Emma, and wanted to know how many would be in the sunroom for dinner. Rafe hadn't returned from out of state yet. But Jack was there. They could make a foursome, have that pinochle rematch.

"Sorry," Cord told her. "Can't make it. I'm going out tonight."

"Hannah, too?"

"I don't know. Why don't you ask her?"

"Cord, is something the matter?"

"Not a thing. Listen, gotta go."

The next day, Kate cornered him in the sunroom, where he was trying to relax with his Sunday paper. She marched right up to him. "Cord, something's going on. I called Hannah last night right after I called you. I asked her to join Jack and me for dinner. She said she couldn't.''

He resolutely did not lower the business section. "So?"

"So…what did that mean, she *couldn't?* I don't get it.''

"Kate. Stay out of it.''

"Stay out of *what?*''

"Hannah's leaving. Monday morning.''

Kate was standing right over him—way too close for comfort. She loomed even closer, so that he couldn't keep the paper high enough to blot out her face. "You can't be serious.''

He reluctantly met her eyes. "I'm deadly serious. She's leaving. And that's all there is to it.''

"But—''

"I mean it, Kate.'' He folded his newspaper and stood. "Leave it alone.''

Her eyes had that mutinous look she got now and then. Kate had a soft heart, but she was definitely a Stockwell. She liked things to go the way she wanted them to go.

He drilled his point home. "Do not—repeat, do not—get involved in this.''

She glared at him.

He glared right back.

She was the one who gave in—with a dramatic exhalation of breath. "Okay, okay. It's your life. You have a right to ruin it your own way, I suppose.''

"Thank you.'' He stuck the business section under his arm and got out of there before she could start in on him again.

The day crawled by. Cord took Becky out alone for a walk on the grounds. He stayed out for two hours. Becky was in model baby mode, cooing and waving her arms happily half the time, sleeping the other half. He went out to the pond and sat on the bench underneath the willow tree. Staring out over the glassy surface where his mother had most likely not drowned after all, he wondered why he wanted to break something, to *hit* something, to make someone pay.

Apparently he was even more like the old man than he'd always thought.

After he took Becky back to the nursery, he went down to the basement and spent an hour and a half in the gym. He gave the heavy punching bag a major workout. It helped.

But only a little.

Sunday night, when he came to Becky's room for her late feeding, Hannah was already there, rocking Becky in the rocker—dressed in khaki slacks and a T-shirt. She was even wearing shoes. He hadn't seen her with her shoes off since the night he'd had her in his bed.

He didn't know why, exactly, but that really got to him. That she took such obvious care against the possibility that he might catch her barefoot now.

The moment he walked in the room, she raised Becky to her shoulder and rose from the rocker. "Here you go." She handed him the baby. "I was just about to get the bottle ready. I'll do it now."

Damned if he'd keep her here if she didn't want to stay. "Don't bother. I can handle it. You can go."

She flashed that phony smile. "All right. Good night, then."

He held Becky's squirming body a little closer and turned away without another word. Hannah went to her room, which infuriated him, though it was only what he'd more or less told her to do. He fed Becky, and changed her, his anger on a short leash through the whole procedure.

Becky seemed to sense the tension in him. She fussed more than usual, and cried when he tried to put her back in her bed. He sat up with her until long after midnight, thinking of all the cruel things he'd like to say to a certain Okie social worker. Then, when Becky finally conked out and he went to bed, he couldn't sleep.

By daylight, he knew he wasn't letting Hannah go without telling her a few of the things he had on his mind.

He liked the new nanny. Mrs. Bridget O'Hara was a plump, good-hearted widow with grown children.

Hannah took her to the nanny's bedroom first, no doubt to drop off her things. Then the two of them came directly to the playroom, where Cord had lingered with his daughter after her morning meal.

Bridget beamed at him and stuck out her very capable looking hand. They shook. Her grip was firm and warm. He knew immediately that Becky would quickly grow to love this woman. The nanny problem had at last been resolved.

He handed Becky to Bridget. She went without a peep. Then he and Bridget talked for a few minutes, while Hannah lurked a few feet away, just waiting for him to get lost.

Too bad. He wasn't going anywhere.

Not until he'd said what he had to say.

He turned to her. "I'll need a few minutes. I'm sure Bridget can handle Becky. Let's just go on over to the sitting room."

Something flashed in those green eyes. Maybe fear— or possibly defiance. But then she nodded. "Of course."

They left the nursery for the room across the hall.

He ushered her in ahead of him, and shut the door once they were both inside. "Have a seat."

She perched on the edge of a leather wing chair. The sight of her there was pure déjà vu. It was the same chair she'd sat in that first day she'd come to stay at the mansion. Exactly two weeks ago now.

Two weeks. Was that all it had been? It seemed to him he had known this woman all his life—and yet, by the same token, their time together felt so brief. The space of a heartbeat.

And now, she was going.

He waited, just looking at her, longer than he should have. He wanted to see if she'd break a little, maybe make a small, nervous sound, shift in her chair—even start talking in that too-cheerful voice she put on whenever she had to deal with him now.

She didn't. She just sat there, waiting, utterly still.

And he remembered. He'd tried silence on her two weeks ago, to see if she'd squirm. It hadn't worked then, either.

Déjà vu all over again, as Yogi Berra would have said.

Best to stop trying to break her. Best to get to the point.

"Time to settle up, Hannah."

She granted him the tiniest of nods.

He'd already made out her check. He took it from his pocket. She gave him the wary-bird treatment, turning her head a little, looking at him sideways.

"Take it. It's only the amount we agreed on. Fourteen days at the rate you named yourself."

Gingerly she held out her hand. He passed her the check. Her shirt had a breast pocket. She stuck it in there without even glancing at it. "Thank you." She stood.

"Not so fast."

She dropped to the edge of the chair again, her composure visibly slipping. "Cord, I don't—"

"This won't take long. Just a few questions."

"What questions?" Her hand flew to her throat. The sight heated his blood.

He *was* getting to her. The thought shouldn't have pleased him as much as it did.

He asked her the most important question—the one that had been eating at him all weekend. "Why are you walking out on me?"

She looked left—and then right. As if by looking anywhere but at him, she could avoid the necessity for a reply.

He pressed on. "I have a theory."

Her gaze snapped back to him again. Her eyes were wide and very worried. He was certain she'd stop him, say she didn't want to hear any theories. That she was leaving. Now.

But she didn't. "All right."

So he laid it on her. "It's revenge, isn't it?"

She shook her head, a quick movement, not in negation—but as if what he'd said made no sense to her. "Revenge? I don't—"

"Are you getting even, damn it?"

She winced and jerked back.

He realized he must have spoken too curtly. He forced himself to breathe, to relax a little, to speak more softly. "Come on. I'm not an idiot—though I have to admit, I've acted like one with you. I can see the parallels, between a rich boy and a wealthy man. A baby you lost—and Becky. You seem to have accepted the fact that Becky stays here, with me. But is there some…satisfaction for you, in dumping me?"

"What?" She looked honestly bewildered. "Satisfaction? In dumping you?"

Impatience knotted his gut. "Yes, Hannah. Dumping me. Walking out on me. Leaving me cold. Are you taking your own brand of revenge, that's what I'm asking, taking it out on me for what some other guy did to you when you were seventeen?''

"No," she said, very low, more a shaping of her lips than a sound. "Oh, Cord." She canted toward him in the chair. "Honestly. No. I told you Thursday night, and I meant it when I said it. I don't want revenge, not in any form, for what happened all those years ago. I truly do not."

"Then what?"

She swallowed, dropped her hand—and immediately raised it to her throat again. "It's...us. Becoming lovers. It shouldn't have happened. It was *wrong*. And I have to make sure it doesn't happen again."

"Why?"

She let out a small sound, something midway between a laugh and a sob. "You *would* ask that. To you, what happened the other night was an everyday occurrence, something you do all the time."

The hell it was, he thought. But he kept his mouth shut. She had it right, up to a point. What they'd done was nothing new to him. It was the way he had *felt* while they were doing it. That had been different.

That had rocked his world.

She went on. "Yes, I'm the one who's doing the leaving here. You're not ready to let go yet. And I'm sorry to hurt you that way. But it's not about revenge. It's about...my dream. My dream for my life. My secret hope for myself, that I've never given up, no matter how bad things got."

She was still leaning toward him, and her eyes were shining now. She looked earnest and infinitely sweet. It was the hardest thing he ever did, not to reach out and pull her into his arms.

"Cord, I want what my parents had. I want *forever*. I want real love, *true* love. With one man. And you've, well, you've said it yourself, and you've said it more than once. Forever is a word you never use."

Was it? Right now, he wasn't so sure. Right now, he would gladly take a run at forever. Hell, he would say anything, *promise* anything, to get her to stay. He would offer it all: the diamond ring, the preacher, the vows ending in "I do."

The words were there, pushing to get out.

Marry me, Hannah. Let's give it a try, at least.

He stepped back.

She was right, damn it.

Never once, until this moment, had he let himself think about forever. He didn't do forever. He was who he was.

Hannah deserved someone better. And as soon as she got away from him, she'd have a chance at finding that someone.

He said, "I'll miss you, Hannah. I'll miss you like hell."

She stood, drawing herself up tall, aiming her chin high. "I'll miss you, too, Cord. You'll never know how much."

Then stay, damn it, he thought. But he didn't let those words get out.

He said, "Goodbye, Hannah. And good luck with that dream of yours."

Chapter Nineteen

On Tuesday, July 3, a week and a day after Hannah moved out of the mansion, a five-page spread appeared in *Inside Scoop* magazine: The Playboy Tycoon And The Unexpected Bundle Of Joy.

The article described Cord's short-lived "liaison" with the unfortunate Marnie Lott. It included the medical particulars of Marnie's early demise, and then went on to wax eloquent about how the wealthy scion of one of Texas' first families had learned he had a child—and immediately took steps to claim the baby he hadn't even realized he'd fathered.

Maya Revere brought the article to Hannah's attention. She read it at her desk at Child Protective Services, during a rare coffee break. The tone, Hannah supposed, could be considered positive. The article made it touchingly clear that the Texas tycoon hadn't hesitated. He'd stepped right up to take responsibility for the unanticipated addition to the Stockwell clan.

Still, Hannah felt certain that Cord would be furious. He'd hate such private stuff to become public knowledge—for Becky's sake, mostly. He wanted the very best for his daughter. And the best did not include having the details of his brief relationship with Becky's mother bandied about in the press.

There were lots of pictures—mostly of Cord at different social functions, dressed to the nines, with various glamorous ex-girlfriends draped over his arm. Looking at those pictures hurt. Hannah knew she had no right at all to think of Cord Stockwell as her personal property, but that didn't stop her from longing to grab each gorgeous woman by her slender throat and strangle her stone dead.

And the pictures of him with all those beautiful women weren't the worst.

Not by a long shot.

The worst were the three photos taken on the mansion grounds—obviously by a hidden photographer. Photos of Cord and Hannah and a baby stroller. Two of the pictures showed them walking side by side along the path beneath the sweet gum trees. And one showed them sitting on the stone bench under the willow by Stockwell Pond.

There was one caption for all three photos: The Playboy, The Baby—And The Nanny. *More* Love In The Air?

That was all. There was nothing in the body of the article linking Hannah and Cord romantically. Her name hadn't even been mentioned. Evidently the reporter hadn't worked very hard to gather his facts—if he had, he probably would have learned that Becky's Child Protective Services worker was the nanny in question. So it could have been worse—or at least, that was what Hannah tried to tell herself.

Once she'd read to the end, she reached for the phone. She had to call Cord, to swear to him that she had never talked to any reporter about him or about Becky.

But she stopped herself.

If he thought she'd had something to do with this, well, so be it. She had no right to call him. She had walked out of his life and she owed it to both of them to stay out.

Her phone rang right then. An emergency, as always. Hannah put Cord from her mind and concentrated on her work.

At Stockwell Mansion, Cord *was* furious. So were Jack and Kate—Rafe was still out of town. The three of them retired to their father's library to discuss whether a lawsuit for invasion of privacy might be the way to go.

Cord, after all, did have a reasonable expectation of privacy when it came to the intimate details of his life. He wasn't running for office and he wasn't an actor; he didn't have the kind of job where a judge might say the very nature of the work he did made his life an open book.

But Jack said, "If we sue, we'll only make the story all the more interesting."

And Cord knew he was right. "What we need to do is find out who let a damn photographer onto the grounds— and then make sure whoever it is never gets a chance to do that again."

Jack said he'd look into it. He wasn't having much luck with his in-depth search of their father's papers. The checks to Clyde Carlyle and the letters from Gabriel Johnson remained their only real leads to whatever had happened in the distant past.

"I'd be glad for the break," Jack said. Then he added, "I hate to say it, but do you think Hannah might have had something to do with this?"

Hannah.

The name ripped through Cord like a serrated knife. He had been trying not to think about her. It was no easy task—especially not right at that moment, with the photos of the two of them in happier times staring him in the face.

"No way." Cord grabbed the open magazine off the library table and tossed it into a nearby wastebasket. The action did nothing to improve the situation, but throwing the thing in the trash provided a surge of satisfaction nonetheless. "Not Hannah," he said. It hurt, just saying her name. "She wouldn't talk to a reporter about Becky. Not in a million years."

Kate backed him up. "Cord's right. That's just not Hannah. It's not Hannah at all."

Jack put up both hands, palms out. "All right, all right. Sorry I suggested it."

Cord moved the discussion along—and away from the subject of the woman he couldn't seem to stop thinking about. "Check with Emma first," he advised Jack. "She handles most of the help. She might know if any of the maids or gardeners have been nosier than they needed to be."

"But be gentle," Kate said.

"Gentle?" Jack was puzzled. "With Emma?"

Kate nodded. "This is the toughest time of the year for her. In case you haven't noticed, the Independence Day party is tomorrow. The poor woman is working practically around the clock."

"She is?"

"Jack, you are *so* oblivious sometimes. There's a band-stand being constructed on the backyard grounds as we speak. And have you noticed the four food tents that are ready to raise? And the barbecue hut? And what about the caterer and the party planner trooping in and out—not to mention that woman from the agency where we get our extra staff, and the guy from the party equipment supply house?''

''Okay, okay. I've noticed that the big party's tomorrow. I just didn't think about the fact that Emma might be under pressure.''

''That's exactly my point. You didn't even consider her.''

''I'm sorry.''

''You should be. Every year, Emma knocks herself out to make everything just right.''

''I wasn't planning to abuse her. I just want to *talk* to her.''

''Gently.''

''I swear it.''

Kate's brows drew together. ''Maybe I ought to give Hannah a call.''

Cord wished he had a muzzle—no, make that *two* muzzles—one for his sister and one for his older brother. What the hell was their problem? Why wouldn't they stop saying her name?

Kate was still talking. ''I don't like the way she just ran out on us and I—''

Cord cut her off before she could finish. ''No.''

''But, Cord, if I could just talk to her, I'm sure she would—''

''Kate, listen. Pay very close attention. No.''

His sister stared at him. He stared right back. Kate blinked first.

''Stay away from her, Kate. Just leave her alone.''

''All right, all right. Whatever you say.''

Kate showed up on Hannah's doorstep at eight the next morning. ''It's the Fourth of July,'' she announced when

Hannah peered around the door at her. "Don't try to tell me that you have to work."

"I'm on call. All the time."

"So unhook the phone. We have to talk."

"Kate—"

"Come on. Let me in. Don't make me stand out here on your cute little porch to say what I have to say."

With a sigh, Hannah pulled the door open all the way. "I knew I should have told the phone company I didn't want my address listed."

"Too late now." Chic as always in fuchsia capris and a funnel neck silk T-shirt, Kate strolled across the threshold. She looked around at Hannah's living room, which had more houseplants than furniture. "This is cozy."

"I like it. Have a seat."

"Don't mind if I do." Kate sank to the sofa and got right down to business. "Cord is miserable. And so are you."

"What? Now you read minds?"

"I don't have to read minds. I can see it in your eyes. And as for my brother, every time someone mentions your name, he looks as if he could kill whoever dared to utter that forbidden word."

Hannah dropped into the Mission-style easy chair she'd bought at a yard sale. "He hates me."

"Oh, please. It's not hate. I promise you it's not."

"Kate, it can't work between Cord and me."

"Why not?"

"Well, he...he's one of the richest men in America."

"Yes. Isn't that lovely? Money isn't everything, but one does learn to live with it."

"Well, all right. I guess you have a point. I could...get used to the money."

"Of course you could."

"But the women, Kate. That's the major thing. He just doesn't have it in him to stay with one woman."

Kate muttered something under her breath. It might have been a swear word, but Hannah couldn't be sure. "Who *says* he doesn't have it in him?"

"*He* says it. Often."

"Oh, wonderful. And you *believe* him?"

Hannah squirmed in the big chair. "I...well, why shouldn't I? He made it very clear to me that he'd never settle down. And then...oh, Kate. There really have been so many women..."

"So? He was looking for the *right* woman."

"I guess so. And it was obviously a worldwide search."

"Hannah, he's not looking anymore."

Hannah knew she must be losing her mind—because she found that Kate was starting to convince her. "You really think so?"

"My brother would hate that I know him so well. But I do. You're the one for him, Hannah. No one else will do. He's a goner. Done for. If you don't go back to him, he'll never find the happiness we both know he deserves."

Hannah spent a number of seconds staring at the shiny leaves of her favorite rubber plant. Finally, she looked at Kate again. "I suppose he's seen that awful article in *Inside Scoop*."

Kate let out a very ladylike snort. "We all saw it."

"I was afraid he might think—"

"Hannah. No way. We know you had nothing to do with that—although I have to admit, it *was* that stupid article that decided me."

"Decided you?"

"To get over here and talk to you. He loves you, Hannah. And I think you love him. Am I right?"

"Oh, Kate…"

"Hannah, don't blow this. Don't throw love away."

Something in Kate's eyes made Hannah long to ask if Cord's sister spoke from experience—but then something else told her that Kate wouldn't answer such a question, anyway.

Kate kicked off her fuchsia wedgies and gathered her feet to the side. "Did you tell him that you love him?"

"Of course not."

"First and major mistake. You'll have to fix that."

"I will?"

"Absolutely. Tell him you love him. And after that, tell him you want to marry him—and if it makes you feel better, tell him he has to promise to give up all the other women for good. Ask him to put it in writing, in a prenup."

"Kate!"

"What?"

"How could you even suggest such a thing? I would never ask for a prenuptial agreement. It says 'forsaking all others' right in the wedding vows. Where I come from, that is more than enough."

"So fine. In any case, you'll have his promise. My brother keeps his promises. I can vouch for that."

"I would never want to force a promise like that out of him."

"Well, all right, Hannah. Then don't. Just…wing it. Just start with 'I love you.' That's all you really need to say anyway. You tell my brother that you love him, and I swear to you, all the rest of it will fall right into place."

Chapter Twenty

"Cord." A slender hand closed over his arm.

He looked up into Jerralyn Coulter's sultry eyes.

They stood in one of the food tents, near a table piled high with tempting delicacies. The Independence Day bash was in full swing. It was shaping up to be the best one ever. Emma had outdone herself. He could hear the band, outside the tent, at the bandstand on the east lawn, not far from the pool. They were playing "The Yellow Rose of Texas."

Jerralyn moved closer. Her scent came with her: musky and expensive. "I've missed you," she murmured, for his ears alone. "I've wanted to call you. But a woman does have her pride..."

She stared up at him with the kind of smoldering look that at one time would have had him inquiring if she'd care to check out the view from his bed/sitting room.

Now, that look did nothing for him—except to inspire a vague feeling of sadness. He missed Hannah.

And damn it, why the hell did every transaction, every interaction, every single thought that went through his head always manage to lead him right back around to Hannah?

Was it always going to be like this?

Damned if he hadn't started to think that it might.

He told Jerralyn, as quietly and kindly as he could, "You flatter me. Don't. Find someone else."

Her smooth brows drew together. "You don't mean that. You've just been…distracted. I heard about your little girl. And I want you to know that I—"

"Jerralyn, I do mean it. Don't."

Her eyes widened. "There's someone else, isn't there?"

He gave her a rueful shrug—and told the truth, though not the whole truth. "I'm afraid so." Jerralyn didn't have to know that he'd lost that someone else.

Jerralyn stared at him for several uncomfortable seconds. Then she muttered something low and crude, tossed her half-filled plate on the table beside them and flounced away.

Cord didn't hang around to watch her go. It was too depressing, that he'd ever been involved with her in the first place. He felt rotten about it.

He felt rotten about all of them, all the women he'd wined and dined and taken to his bed and eventually grown tired of. What the hell had been the point? He didn't even remember anymore.

He just wanted Hannah. To talk to her. To hear her laugh. To walk with her under the sweet gum trees…

He left the tent, which was air-conditioned, for the sweltering Texas heat outside. Emma had mist-makers going, of course, all over the grounds, devices that spewed a fine, cool spray. They helped, cooling the skin as the mist evaporated. But this *was* summer in Texas, after all. A man could air-condition his house and his party tents. But there was only so much that could be done about the great outdoors.

Cord grinned to himself, thinking that maybe, on second thought, he'd just mosey right back into that cool tent.

He was just about to turn, when he saw her.

She stood twenty yards away, wearing a sleeveless lemon-yellow dress that skimmed her curves and ended just above her pretty knees. She was talking to Kate. They were laughing together...

What the hell? It wasn't enough that he thought of her constantly? Now he'd begun to hallucinate that he was actually *seeing* her?

Must be the heat.

He shut his eyes, counted to three and opened them again.

She was still there.

My God, he thought. She's real.

Right then, a hand closed on his shoulder. "Cord. Great party. You Stockwells have done it again."

He started to jerk away—and caught himself just in time. "Senator, glad you could come..."

It took him a good two minutes to get away from the politician. And by then, Hannah—and Kate—had vanished. He went looking, following the winding path under the trees. It wasn't long until he found her again—or he thought he did. He saw a flash of yellow at the entrance to the formal gardens.

He followed after, moving fast, though she had disappeared around a bend in the path. He walked even faster, catching up just enough that he saw her again.

Definitely. Hannah.

He said the name aloud. "Hannah."

She stopped. And she turned.

And damn it if she didn't smile.

He moved toward her, feeling as if he walked in some dream, never letting go of her eyes, sure that if he did, she would vanish again.

When he reached her side, he realized that he didn't have a clue what to say. She was just so beautiful, in that yellow dress, with her chestnut hair shining in the spots of sunlight that filtered down through the trees.

And he felt...

There was only one word for it: shy. He couldn't believe it. Never in his life had he been shy with a woman.

"Will you walk with me?" He offered his arm.

And she took it. The feel of her, brushing against him, and the touch of her hand on his arm, was everything to him. Nothing had ever meant so much.

They went on, through the garden, out under the rose arbor gate, and onto the lawn that sloped down to the pond.

"It's so hot," she said. "Let's go out and sit on the dock. We can take off our shoes and put our feet in the water."

Take off our shoes...

He hardly dared to breathe. She would take off her shoes in his presence again.

That had to be a good sign, didn't it?

He followed where she led him, to the end of the dock, where he dropped down beside her. He got rid of his shoes and socks and rolled up his slacks as she shucked off her yellow sandals. Together, they swung their feet out over the water.

Their toes barely touched the surface. It was a hot summer, and would get hotter. The water level dropped just a little every day.

"It's a reach," she said, laughing. She dipped her toe in, scooping up water drops, sending them splashing. He drank in her laughter. He was a drowning man, going under, into those shining leaf-green eyes...

He leaned toward her a little, and she leaned toward him. "Hannah..."

"Yes, Cord?"

"Hannah, I—"

The sound of footsteps rushing toward them down the dock cut him off before he could get out the crucial words.

They turned together. Yolanda, one of the day maids, hurried toward them. "Mr. Cord, Mr. Caine is calling for you. He is very bad. He wants you to come to him. Right away."

He almost said no. Forget it. Let him holler all he wants, I'm not leaving this dock. I'm not leaving this woman...

He *couldn't* leave her. If he did, she might just disappear from his life all over again.

She leaned even closer to him. The scent of her taunted him. How had he lived without her—the sight of her, the *smell* of her...

"Go on," she said. "I'll wait for you in Becky's room...if that's all right?"

Somehow, he managed to nod. "Yes. All right. Becky's room. I won't be long."

"Take as long as you need."

Caine was shouting when Cord entered his rooms. "I want my son! Where the hell is my son?"

Cord went right to him, sent the nurses away, and listened to him rant and rail.

He tried, once he got Caine settled down just a little, to get some scrap of new information about Madelyn and Brandon, and about the land deal. Caine wouldn't even reply when Cord tried to prod him into saying something about the letters from Gabriel Johnson.

But the old man did mutter, "You'll have to ask Clyde Carlyle," when Cord asked about Madelyn.

Eventually Caine closed his eyes and drifted off into a fitful slumber. Cord rang for the nurses.

Jack, Kate and Rafe were waiting out in the hallway when he left his father's suite.

Kate said, "Look who's home."

Cord lifted an eyebrow at Rafe. "About time, little brother."

Rafe shrugged. "Hannah told Kate you'd been called by the old man. Is he all right?"

"No," said Cord. "But he's not dying. Not today, anyway."

"Did you get anything new out of him?"

"He mentioned Clyde Carlyle by name. Said we should ask him, if we wanted to know where Madelyn was."

"Anything else?"

"Sorry. That's all."

Jack spoke then. "I've got some news. We found out who let the photographer onto the grounds. It was one of the gardeners. The head gardener caught him out by the north gate a couple of weeks ago, a place he had no business being. The head gardener mentioned the strange behavior to Emma, and she remembered it when I talked to her. I had a few words with the man in question. He confessed that he'd taken five thousand dollars to sneak a photographer through the gate."

"He's fired," said Cord.

Jack nodded. "I escorted him out personally."

Rafe looked confused. Quickly Kate filled him in on what had happened in his absence.

Once he had the story, Rafe said, "Good work, Jack."

Jack grunted. "It's a hell of a lot better than I've done trying to gather more clues about Gabriel Johnson—not to mention the fates of our mother and uncle and possible brother or sister."

"Time to take action," Rafe said. "I'll talk to Caroline tomorrow."

Kate was grinning. "And you, Cord Stockwell, had better head for the nursery. Someone special is waiting there."

Cord detoured to his bedroom, briefly. Then he went to the nursery, where he found Hannah with his daughter in her arms. She passed the baby to Bridget and shyly held out her hand.

"Let's go to the sitting room."

They went across the hall and into the room where he'd first asked her to take care of his daughter, the room where they'd said their "final" goodbyes. He didn't offer her a seat this time. Instead he pulled her into his arms and kissed her, long and hard and thoroughly.

Finally, breathlessly, she pulled away—but only to look up at him with those shining eyes and declare, "I love you, Cord. With all of my heart. And...I'm so sorry I left you. I was just so afraid. To give my heart. To take a chance it might get broken again."

He wanted to tell her that he understood, it was all right—as long as she swore she was here to stay now.

He started to speak, to say those important things. But she put her soft fingers against his lips. "I want you to know. I've learned something. I've learned that I don't want to live without you if I don't have to—not without you *or* without Becky. And I want to ask, if there's any chance in the world that you might feel the same way…''

He opened his mouth again—to tell her exactly how he felt.

But she said, ''Shh. Wait. I…''

''Damn it, Hannah. What?''

''I was wondering if, maybe, we could start again. Take it slowly. I wouldn't expect marriage, not at first. I would want to give you time to get used to the idea of being tied down. Maybe it wouldn't be so hard for you as you think it would be. After all, you've turned out to be such a very fine father, when I know you were real nervous about that at the first. Maybe you'll find out that…'' She seemed unsure of how to go on.

He couldn't help smiling. He knew it was a pretty smug smile. ''Maybe I'll find out what?''

Her sweet face was a warm pink. ''Oh, I am making a darn fool of myself. I just…wanted to say that I am in love with you, Cord Stockwell. That I'd like to try to make a life with you.''

''You would?''

Hannah gazed up at him, at this man that she loved. He was smiling at her, one of those devastating smiles of his—the kind that stole her breath right out of her chest and made her heart pound so hard it felt like it just might explode.

He took a box from his pocket—a small blue one tied with a white ribbon—and he handed it to her. With slow care, she untied the ribbon. There was a little blue pouch inside. And inside that pouch, a pin. A pin shaped like a starfish. It was studded with round blue stones and had a blood-red ruby right at its center.

''It's not a ring,'' he said, sounding so sweet and regretful. "If I'd known you were coming back today, I would have gotten you a ring."

"I love it."

"You do?"

She couldn't resist slanting him a look of teasing suspicion. "But what about my nightgown?"

"You can have it whenever you want it—as long as you only wear it for me."

She did like the sound of that. "Only for you," she whispered, staring into his eyes. "Help me..."

He pinned the starfish to the shoulder of her dress and declared with tender solemnity, "I love you, too, Hannah. More than you'll ever know. And it took me a while to figure it all out, but I understand now. It doesn't matter what my father did, the mistakes he made, the love he never really found. I don't have to be like him. I can give you my word and know I will keep it. There's not going to be anyone else, Hannah. How could there be, now that there's you?"

She gazed up at him, her heart full to bursting with pure joy.

He went on. "I want marriage. With you. I'm not going to settle for anything less. And I want it soon. I don't want to waste another minute of my life without you at my side. Will you marry me, Hannah?"

She did not have the words to say what was in her heart. So she simply continued to gaze at him, all of her love in her eyes.

"Damn it, say yes."

So she did, with feeling. "Yes, Cord. Oh, yes."

It was all Cord Stockwell needed to hear. He pulled her close and lowered his mouth to hers, thinking as he kissed her that a miracle had occurred. Somehow, in the process of claiming a daughter he hadn't even realized existed, he had stumbled onto happiness. Happiness in the form of Ms. Hannah Waynette Miller, the only woman in the world who could turn the Lone Star State's most notorious playboy tycoon into a man with forever on his mind.

Epilogue

Later, as fireworks blazed in the Texas sky, Rafe Stockwell watched his twin and Hannah.

Cord stood behind his bride-to-be, his arms wrapped around her. Hannah glanced back at him. The two exchanged the kind of look only those long-gone in love can share.

For some reason, that look had Rafe thinking of Caroline Carlyle, though why the hell it should was a mystery to him. The woman had dumped him, after all.

Still, he had to admit, at least to himself, that he felt some…anticipation, at the thought of seeing her again. And he was curious, too, to meet the man she'd dumped him for, the one she'd said she planned to be spending a lot of time with in the future.

Tomorrow, he thought, turning from the lights exploding in the sky. Tomorrow, he'd drop in at the offices of Carlyle and Carlyle.

And he and Caroline could have a nice, long talk.

*   *   *   *   *

Turn the page for a sneak preview of the next

STOCKWELLS OF TEXAS *novel*

*Look for Rafe Stockwell and
Caroline Carlyle's story in*

SEVEN MONTHS AND COUNTING...

By Myrna Temte

*Coming your way from
Silhouette Special Edition
On sale February 2001*

Available at your favorite retail outlet

Chapter One

Good God, she was pregnant.

Deputy U.S. Marshal Rafe Stockwell came to an abrupt halt inside the doorway to the offices of Carlyle and Carlyle in Grandview, Texas. Crushing the brim of the pearl-gray Stetson hat he carried in his left hand, he rocked back on his boot heels and stared at his former lover, Ms. Caroline Carlyle, Attorney-at-Law. She stood beside a large, jumbled stack of boxes at the far end of the reception area, checking something off on a clipboard, her concentration so intense she didn't notice him.

It was a darn good thing, too. He needed the time to close his mouth. He couldn't believe the change in her appearance. She'd been sleek and chic when she'd dumped him three months and twenty-nine days ago. Not that he'd been counting.

Now, here she was, filling out a maternity dress and wearing plain black flats instead of the sexy high heels he'd always loved. And her sunshine-yellow hair had been cut into a short, puffy style that curled under just below her jawline. It looked attractive on her, but he'd loved playing with her long, silky hair so much, he felt a twinge of sadness at the thought of anyone taking scissors to it.

He'd never had a thing for pregnant ladies before, but Caroline still was one of the most beautiful women he'd ever seen. In his eyes, the pregnancy had actually enhanced her looks. It had softened her features somehow, made her seem less perfect, warmer and more approachable. An invisible hand wrapped around his heart and squeezed it hard.

He was hardly an expert on pregnant women, but the way her belly was hanging right out there, he wondered just how far along she was. Five months? Six? Maybe even seven?

She flipped the top page on her clipboard, then heaved a dispirited sigh. Rubbing the small of her back as if it ached, she closed her eyes and rolled her head from side to side. She looked tired, as if the baby she carried already was too heavy for her slender frame.

An urge to protect her and take care of her surged inside Rafe. Gritting his teeth, he reminded himself that she was only a friend these days; her well-being now was another man's responsibility. Her pregnancy had nothing to do with him.

Or did it?

The hair on the back of Rafe's neck zinged a warning to his nervous system. Whoa. Wait just a minute. Back up there a thought or two.

He blinked, then focused his gaze on Caroline's belly again. *Five, six or seven* months? If any of those numbers was right, it would mean that the baby she was carrying could be——

No. No, it couldn't. She would have told him. He was sure of it. Nevertheless his heart suddenly revved faster than one of his twin brother Cord's pricey little sports cars and the strangest sensation invaded Rafe's insides. He shut his eyes and raked his right hand through his hair, but the thought he'd always considered unthinkable echoed in his mind.

What if that baby was *his?*

He'd been mighty careful about birth control, but the only truly foolproof method was abstinence, and he sure hadn't practiced *that* with Caroline. Making love with her had been... He wasn't going to think about that just now. He needed to use his head and keep other, more unruly parts of his anatomy under control.

Besides, there was no sense jumping to any wild conclusions.

Caroline didn't have "accidents." Shoot, she was almost as much of a control freak as he was, and this was Texas, not Hollywood. No way would she allow herself to get pregnant without a husband around to make everything nice and socially acceptable. Rafe hadn't heard anything about her getting married, but he'd been working a lot. And because of her father's battle with Alzheimer's disease, she might have decided to have a small, quiet wedding.

So what if she was really big? Maybe she was carrying twins. Maybe twins ran in her husband's family. The same way they did in his own.

Oh, God. What if that baby really *was* his?

"Aw, jeez," he muttered, shoving his fingers through his hair again.

Caroline started at the sound of his voice, then whipped her head around and stared at him. Her blue eyes widened in what looked like pleasure when she first caught sight of him. A heartbeat later her expression changed to one of shock, which was quickly covered by a mask of professional courtesy. She straightened her shoulders and raised her chin, presenting him with the poised image he'd come to expect from her. Nothing flustered Ms. Caroline Carlyle for long.

"Rafe, what a nice surprise," she said. "It's been a long time."

Rafe had to smile. He'd forgotten how much her proper little Boston accent tickled him. Her folks should have let her come home to Texas from that Massachusetts boarding school more often.

"It sure has, Caroline." He walked father into the suite of offices, glancing at her belly, then shifting his attention to her face. "Well, I guess congratulations are in order."

She sidestepped a box and came toward him. Pregnant or not, with or without high heels, she still had the sexiest legs and the greatest walk in Texas.

"Thank you, Rafe." She offered him her right hand. "What can I do for you today?"

Still reeling from the possible implications of her pregnancy, Rafe could barely remember his own name, much less the original reason for his visit. He tossed his partially mangled hat onto the reception desk and shook her hand, then instinctively reached for her left hand and lifted it up beside her right one. Her fingers felt small and fragile in his.

She wore a plain gold wedding band.

Rafe swallowed hard, telling himself he felt relief that she was married to somebody else, not regret. Rubbing his thumbs over the backs of her fingers, he cleared his throat and raised his gaze to meet hers. "Who's the lucky guy?"

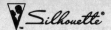

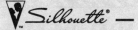

Silhouette ®

where love comes alive—online...

eHARLEQUIN.com

shop eHarlequin

- ♥ Find all the new Silhouette releases at everyday great discounts.

- ♥ Try before you buy! Read an excerpt from the latest Silhouette novels.

- ♥ Write an online review and share your thoughts with others.

reading room

- ♥ Read our Internet exclusive daily and weekly online serials, or vote in our interactive novel.

- ♥ Talk to other readers about your favorite novels in our Reading Groups.

- ♥ Take our Choose-a-Book quiz to find the series that matches you!

authors' alcove

- ♥ Find out interesting tidbits and details about your favorite authors' lives, interests and writing habits.

- ♥ Ever dreamed of being an author? Enter our Writing Round Robin. The Winning Chapter will be published online! Or review our writing guidelines for submitting your novel.